Happy Holidays:
A Political Thriller

J.D. Smith

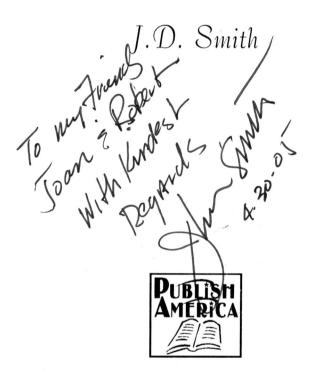

PublishAmerica
Baltimore

© 2005 by J. D. Smith.
All rights reserved. No part of this book may be reproduced, stored in a retrieval system or transmitted in any form or by any means without the prior written permission of the publishers, except by a reviewer who may quote brief passages in a review to be printed in a newspaper, magazine or journal.

First printing

ISBN: 1-4137-4861-9
PUBLISHED BY PUBLISHAMERICA, LLLP
www.publishamerica.com
Baltimore

Printed in the United States of America

Is it possible? Could the unthinkable really happen…a terrorist elected President of the United States? Yes, that is, unless James Wright solves the Happy Holiday's riddle!

This novel is a work of fiction. The characters, names, incidents, dialogue, and plot are the products of the author's imagination or are used fictitiously. Any resemblance to actual persons, organizations or events is purely coincidental.

Dedication

I want to express my gratitude to my family and friends, especially to my parents J.V. and Clotielde Smith, for their continuing support throughout this storytelling endeavor. Their faith has inspired me through the completion of this book.

My wife, and partner in life, Billie Kay, is my first and most critical reader. I thank her for her strong opinions and encouragement. Her love has given me the opportunity to freely pursue my dreams.

To my brother Bill, I am indebted for the joy he has instilled in me for writing.

Through his mentoring, I have gained confidence in my ability as an author.

Finally, to the wonderful professionals at A-1 Editing: Editor-in-Chief Nicole Bentley and especially, Senior Editor Rusty Fischer. They are truly among the best in the literary field. Without their expertise and guidance, this manuscript would be incomplete.

Thank you so much.

Prologue

Reprinted with permission from *Stars and Stripes*, Vol. 1: Issue 76:

WAS A FOX GUARDING THE ARMY'S HEN HOUSE?

On April 5, 1992, the United States Military Court in Leavenworth, Kansas, sentenced a distinguished American soldier and Congressional Medal of Honor recipient, U.S. Army Colonel Jacob "Jake" Stahl, to ten years in prison. The pronouncement followed a months-long court martial and eventual conviction that found Stahl guilty of accepting bribes, money laundering, and various and sundry fraudulent dealings with corrupt government officials in Europe, the Middle East, and Mexico. Although never proven conclusively, prosecutors alleged that his various financial dealings involved what they termed "organized terrorist cells," including the infamous Al Qaida.

Ironically, at the time of his arrest, Stahl commanded a U.S. Army Special Operatives anti-terrorist unit deployed around the world to investigate the same type crimes for which he was eventually tried and convicted.

Throughout the trial, Stahl and his attorneys maintained an unwavering plea of innocence, claiming a "set-up" by the very people he had investigated in his role as terrorist watchdog. In the end, it was a preponderance of circumstantial evidence, however, that linked Stahl to numerous criminal acts and ultimately convinced the military court of his guilt.

Those who knew Stahl best described his demise as, "An American tragedy…a stellar military career that flickered, dimmed and ultimately burned out."

Others, including a superior officer, Major General Douglas Wood, felt that "…justice had been served." In a statement following the court sentence, General Wood said, "It is disappointing and certainly disconcerting that an individual with significant career achievements and responsibilities has been found guilty of these types of crimes. Still, there must be a standard—a consequence—especially for those in whom the United States has placed its greatest trust."

Ultimately, the conviction cost Stahl everything that had ever held any significance for the career colonel. Within weeks of his sentencing, Stahl's wife, Sarah, filed for divorce, took custody of their twelve-year-old daughter and changed their legal names. Five years after his incarceration, Stahl's father, a former military career officer, passed away. Some said he never overcame the heartache he felt for his son. Following the loss of her husband, the health of Stahl's mother quickly deteriorated as well. Grief stricken and without any immediate family, she eventually became despondent. Months later, she passed away in a nursing home, a virtual invalid.

Ten years later, following his release from prison, Stahl picked up the pieces of his broken life. But, initially, a lack of money relegated him to the life of a derelict. For weeks, he moved nomadically from one town to another, finding work where he could, living hand to mouth.

A shadow of his former self...

Instinctively, he made his way to California, where he'd spent most of his life and military career. Strangely, the west coast offered hope and, perhaps one day, the opportunity to even the score with those he still held responsible for his dramatic and costly downfall.

But most of all, Jake Stahl wanted anonymity; Jake Stahl wanted seclusion. Jake Stahl wanted time to contemplate, time to ponder and time to plan. Jake Stahl wanted a haven, and he found that haven in the City of Angels: Los Angeles, California.

At the time of this reporting, Stahl had "no comment" about his past, his present, or most noticeably, his future. Apparently, the terrorists he once worked so hard to prosecute weren't the only ones adept at flying under society's radar.

* * * * * *

Ten Years Later...

La Ciudad de Los Angeles.
Los Angeles County, California.

The City of Angels. In the classic television detective series *Dragnet,* Jack Webb called it merely, "The City." Today, Los Angeles is one of the nation's largest metropolitan areas. Home to some 9,802,800 souls, LA sprawls across four thousand eighty one square miles, featuring eighty miles of Pacific coastline and a landmass bigger than Delaware and Rhode Island combined.

Beverly Hills. Hollywood. Long Beach. Malibu. Pasadena. South Central LA. Thanks to television and the movies, these are all household names among the annals of California history; eclectic communities where expansive beaches, professional sports teams, and world-class entertainment promote a jet-setting, fast-paced lifestyle.

Interestingly, the University of California at Los Angeles, California State, and California Poly Tech attract the best and brightest minds in the world—scholars, doctors, scientists and Nobel Prize winners. In contrast, the Dodgers, Angels and Lakers, in their inevitable quest for national championships, draw sports enthusiasts from around the world. In between, of course, and occasionally even blurring the lines between academia, sports stardom, and *real* stardom is the make-believe world of Hollywood, where movie stars and famous personalities offer a contradiction between fantasy and the realities of every day life.

There is a dark side, though, to this sun-soaked, palm-lined slice of fantasy Americana. An underbelly you don't read about in the *Los Angeles Chamber of Commerce Annual Report*.

In 1965 and 1992, riots in LA rocked the country and reminded us of the pervasiveness of poverty, hate and racism in "The City of Angels." In 1995, the O.J. Simpson trial fragmented the judicial confidence of our nation, raising the issues of legal malpractice and police ineptness that still reverberate through court trials, not to mention Court TV, to this day.

In 2000 a scandal involving LAPD officers darkened the fallen shadow of authority figures, public officials, and national leaders alike. Each is a tattered page among the the pulp fiction—and nonfiction—annals of LA's tarnished history.

But life in a big city *has* its appeal; its personality is an elixir from which even the most wary can be seduced like farm-fed co-eds from the Midwest at LA's notoriously dangerous bus stations.

Buried deep within this complex nature is a world where anonymity finds seclusion. A place where criminals, fugitives, derelicts—the *down and outs*—blend quickly into its faceless environment.

Following his release from prison, Jake Stahl wanted to *blend*. Jake Stahl wanted anonymity and seclusion. Jake Stahl wanted time. Time to contemplate.

Time to plan ...

* * * * * *

Thursday, June 6, 2002, 10:15 a.m.
Los Angeles, California

"Okay, Elizabeth, time for bed. Give your mom a kiss goodnight!"
"Oh, Daddy, do I *have* to go to bed now? I'm not even tired yet!"
"I know, little girl. You're *never* tired! Go...kiss your mom. I'll read you a story."

Dressed in pajamas, Elizabeth stood from the bedroom floor where she was playing with her *Barbie*. Grasping the toy figurine with both hands, she kissed it tenderly on the cheek. As she walked toward her bed, she spoke to the doll with animation, placing it lovingly against her pillow.

"It's time to go to bed, *Barbie*! Daddy says we have to go to bed now!"

Turning quickly, the little girl dashed past her Dad, who stood in the bedroom doorway. Listening carefully, he could hear the sound of her tiny feet running down the hallway to her mother's bedroom.

"Sarah!" he called. "Elizabeth's coming to give you a kiss goodnight!"

"Okay, *Daddy*," came the distant reply of the little girl's mother.

Moments later, Elizabeth raced into the bedroom. As she whizzed past her father, she jumped onto the bed and pulled back the covers.

"Okay, Daddy. I'm ready. Will you read *Cinderella*?"

"*Cinderella*?!?" he queried, acting as though he was not familiar with the title.

"Hmm," he pondered, smiling wryly as he walked to her bed, "have we read that one before?"

"Oh, Daddy! You *know* that's my favorite story!" the little girl retorted with exasperation.

"Oh yes, *now* I remember! Why don't we read *Cinderella*! Hey, how about scootin' over... gimme some room! Don't be such a '*bed hog*'!"

Giggling, the little girl wiggled toward the center of the bed as her daddy took his place beside her, leaning back against the pillow. Elizabeth snuggled against his side as he opened the storybook and began to read aloud the words the little girl loved so well. Both were tired and before long, fast asleep.

As she prepared for bed, Sarah checked Elizabeth's bedroom. Peering into the room from the hallway, she smiled admiringly at her husband and daughter, snuggled together like peas in a pod.

Quietly, she tiptoed to the bedside, kissed them on their foreheads, and turned out the light ...

* * * * * *

What's that sound, he thought. *That noise...that pounding...Sarah...Elizabeth...?*

Am I dreaming...Sarah...Elizabeth? The bedtime story seemed real, so alive...yet—

"Where am I?"

The incessant pounding seemed louder. With each blow, Jake Stahl felt as if his head would explode.

"How long have I been asleep? One day...two?"

"And the drinking? How much had I consumed?" He had no idea. All he knew was that his head was *killing* him!

Since his release from prison six weeks earlier, time passed without measure or distinction... one day... two days... a week. Only the liquor had numbed his anguish.

The pounding continued. This time he realized it was not his head after all, but the sound of someone knocking on the front door.

Lying on the couch of the living room, he tried to make sense of what was happening. He was a wreck—hair disheveled, face unshaven. Wearing only an undershirt and wrinkled slacks, his belt was loosened at the waist. He wore no shoes.

From the self-induced stupor, Jake strained to open one bloodshot eye, then both. The room was a spinning blur. God, his head hurt.

He blinked and squinted his eyes to focus. On the coffee table, an arms-length away, he recognized the shape of a familiar bottle—Jack Daniels, near empty. No drinking glass, just the bottle. Now his head *really* hurt as he realized just how much whiskey he had consumed.

Next to the bottle, like bookends, were his wallet and wristwatch. For several moments he stared at the piece of jewelry. Slowly, his shaking hand moved to grasp the golden timekeeper.

He blinked again until the dial was in focus. "Ten- fifteen... 10:15...a.m. or p.m.? Ten-fifteen." The sunlight streaming through the window told him it was morning. With the next series of knocks, a voice beckoned.

"Colonel Stahl!"

"Colonel *Jacob* Stahl!"

A minute passed before he answered.

"Yes ..."

There was no reply.

He struggled to sit upright, then finally stand. His legs felt weak and unstable from the effects of the liquor. Slowly, he grasped the corner of the sofa for balance and made his way across the room.

With every step across the room, he clung to pieces of furniture like a crutch. Still, he bumped the edge of a chair as he moved toward the front door.

Reaching the doorway, he extended his right arm for balance and braced himself against the living room wall. Slowly, the fingers of his left hand fumbled to grasp the knob of the deadbolt. He rotated the handle a quarter turn and unlocked the door.

Leaning against the doorframe, his left hand turned the doorknob. Carefully, he pulled on the hardware and opened the door. Instantly, the bright California sunlight streaming through the opening blinded him. Instinctively, he lifted his left arm in front of his face to shield his bloodshot eyes from the piercing rays.

Blinking his eyes, he tried to focus, this time, on the person standing on the porch in front of him. Squinting, he took note of his appearance.

There, standing three feet away, was a man. At first glance, he looked to be in his early thirties. A dark gray suit, fashionable shirt, tie and polished shoes gave him the look of a dynamic, upcoming professional. Wire-framed glasses and a thin, black leather briefcase tucked under his left arm enhanced the image. But, then again, looks could be deceiving. Without hesitation, the stranger began to speak.

"Colonel Stahl, my name is John Bradford. I am an associate for a legal firm that represents the estate of your deceased parents. In their will, they named the firm as estate executor."

My parents, he thought. *How I miss them.* Both had died while he was in prison. Sadly, their once-strong spirits were eventually broken by the events of his life. As disheartened as they were, however, they never abandoned him.

Throughout his life, Jake had admired his father—a decorated World War II veteran who always put family first. He was a father who idolized his only son. Less than five years ago, he passed away, having never overcome the grief and disillusionment of the court martial.

Several months later he received word of his mother's depression, illness, and subsequent death. What a lady. Stalwart, she cared deeply for her family. The countless moves around the world never daunted her love or the support she gave to her husband and his career.

"Colonel," the young man continued with massive understatement, "I see that you are not feeling well, but the information I have to share will not take but a moment of your time. As a part of the estate, your parents willed the proceeds of their savings and investments to you. It seems your father was quite successful in his financial affairs.

"Over his lifetime the value of these investments has grown considerably. The *World Banc* account in Zurich in which these monies are deposited has a fund balance of more than two million dollars!"

For a brief moment the lawyer's words registered in his drug-induced state-of-mind. But the stranger continued to speak, distracting his strained attempt to comprehend what was being said. As the man spoke, he unzipped the leather brief tucked beneath his arm. From one of its sleeves he removed a file folder and a plain, letter-size envelope.

"To establish the account under your name, there are two documents for your signature. One is your acknowledgment as owner of the account. The second validates your account's Personal Identification Number or PIN."

"The PIN," explained the lawyer, "along with the password that you select, will activate the account."

Carefully, the man positioned the documents on the back of the leather brief and without deliberation, removed a ballpoint pen from the inside lapel pocket of his coat. Clicking the instrument with his thumb to a writing position, he extended the items arms-length to the Colonel.

"Colonel, if you will sign here," pointing to the signature line on the first document, "and here," indicating the second, "I'll be on my way."

"This," gesturing to the plain envelope, "contains your copy of the transaction."

Instinctively, Jake Stahl grasped the pen and, with shaking hand, signed his name. Having completed the task, he looked, without speaking, at the face of the young man. For a moment, their eyes met.

The lawyer returned the signed documents to the leather brief, speaking again as he closed its zipper. "Thank you, Colonel. If you should have any questions, there is additional information in the envelope."

Turning away, the stranger negotiated the steps of the porch, moved quickly down the sidewalk to the street, and was gone.

Standing there, confused and alone on the porch, Jake Stahl struggled to recount the words of the stranger. "Estate...will...*World Banc* account...two million dollars." He glanced at the envelope and clutched it with his hands. Feeling its texture confirmed the reality of the encounter. But still he wondered, "What was this all about?" He didn't know ...

Suddenly, the lingering effects of the alcohol, heightened by the heat of the morning sun, enveloped him. Becoming increasingly disoriented, he began to perspire profusely, a wave of nausea coursing through his frail body. Turning around, he braced his hand against the outside wall, opened the door, and went inside.

Placing his right hand against the wall of the hallway, he balanced himself. Slowly, he made his way down the corridor to the master bedroom. Pausing momentarily at the doorway, he staggered through the room to the bath. His head was pounding.

In the medicine chest above the lavatory was a bottle of aspirin. Positioning the envelope under his right arm, he opened the cabinet.

Grasping the bottle with his left hand, he popped the safety cap of the container with his thumb and poured four tablets into the palm of his right hand.

On the counter, next to the lavatory, was an empty glass. Turning the faucet handle, he filled the glass, tossed the tablets into his mouth, and chased the medicine down his throat with the water.

Returning to the bedroom, he opened the closet door. On the top shelf above his clothes was a cardboard box in which he stored papers and personal documents. Lifting its lid, he placed the envelope inside.

Having completed the task, Jake turned to the bed, walked several steps to its edge and collapsed lengthwise across the mattress. Within moments, he was asleep.

* * * * * *

Four Months Later ...

He read the headline again slowly, for the third time, focusing on every word. It was not a front-page story; rather a single column buried pages deep in the first section. Still, it caught his attention—something personal, something to which he could relate:

Senator Remains Bitter in Defeat – *Months after his failed attempt to win the Presidency, California Senator Richard Davis remains bitter from his close election defeat to President George Stone. In a recent interview, the Senator criticized the President for his homeland security plan and the deployment of Voyeur.*

Stone underscored his bitterness with a statement implying the possibility, in four years, of another run for the highest office in the land. The White House refused comment about the Senator's statements.

How badly did the Senator want to become President? How much would he be willing to pay? Perhaps he just might find out...

* * * * * *

Tuesday, April 6, 2004, 2:00 A.M.
Washington, D.C.

Finally, after what seemed like an eternity to the young staff officer, the persistent ring of the telephone pierced the deep sleep of General James Wright. Startled by the call, James groped the darkness for the handset next to his bed. Blinking, he oriented himself, then answered: "Yes?"

"General, sir. I'm sorry to disturb you, sir."

The familiar, but apologetic voice always followed protocol. Both knew the disruption was inherent to their job.

"Yes, Lieutenant. What is it?"

"Sir, we've had an event—in Tel Aviv."

"Tel Aviv?" What the hell's going on there?"

"Appears to be an ordinance, sir—some type of bomb. The device exploded in the city…downtown…about thirty minutes ago."

"Bomb? Where did *that* damn thing come from?"

"We don't know, sir. There was no warning. No intelligence. Nothing."

"*Jesus Christ!* What else?"

"Sir, there are casualties, both civilian and military; possibly NATO and Israeli government personnel. We don't have the numbers yet…"

"You said there was no warning? No advance intelligence? What about *Voyeur*?"

"Nothing, sir. Nothing from *Voyeur*, nothing at all. Sir?"

"Yes."

"Sir, if I may speak freely, the event is similar to the Dublin hit

last month."
"Yes, I understand. Send me what you have. Use the secure line. Follow the protocol. I'll download the report and call the Secretary."
"Yes, sir."
"And Lieutenant?"
"Yes, sir."
"Notify the chiefs. I'll meet them at the Pentagon in one hour...and send a car over."
"Yes, sir. Is there anything else, sir?"
"That's all for now, Lieutenant. Thank you."
"Sir?"
"Yes, Lieutenant."
"Sir, if I might ask?"
"Yes, what is it?"
"Sir... what do you think?"

James paused, pondering the lieutenant's question before he replied, "I don't know, Lieutenant. I just don't know."

* * * * * *

Tuesday, April 6, 2004. 2:05 a.m.
Washington, D.C.

A 2:00 a.m. wake up call to anyone other than General James Wright would have been an interloper. But long ago, James lost count of the disruptions to his daily life. Time schedules are meaningless to those whose workplace is a global environment. Fortunately, his wife Susan was in Chicago visiting her sister. Otherwise, she would be sharing this often-repeated event.

Keenly alert now, the general made his way to the kitchen and turned on the light. Walking to the coffee maker, he switched the *auto* setting to *manual*. Spontaneously, the indispensable appliance responded noisily as it regurgitated its addictive dark-brown elixir into the angular glass carafe.

Retracing his steps, he moved quickly through the master bedroom to the shower. Soon, clouds of water droplets from the steaming vapor collected on the bathroom mirror and walls. This morning there was no time for leisure. Every passing minute was critical.

From his office down the hall, the dial-up indicator on the fax machine beeped. Simultaneously, the audio prompt on his computer signaled "incoming mail." The details of these messages would direct his upcoming conversation with the secretary of defense.

James felt no anxiety in making the call. His concern was for those impacted by the tragedy. Certainly, it would be stressful for the secretary and the President. But their role as world leaders demanded they be fluent with the political and military fallout from catastrophic events. It was a responsibility they understood; it *came with the territory.*

Following the quick shower, James sat half-dressed on the edge of the bed as he pored over the details of the intelligence report. When he had sorted out the sequence of events, he pressed the speed-dial button on the telephone. The call would connect him with one of the highest-ranking officials in the United States. Moments later, the secretary himself answered.

"Yes."

"Frank?"

"Yes, Jim." After years of a lasting friendship and shared tours of duty in the armed service, both men recognized the familiar voices on the other end of the line.

"Frank, we've had an incident in Tel Aviv... about an hour ago. Intelligence reports some type of ordinance in the downtown square."

"Damn, Jim! What's this all about?"

"Right now, I don't know. It appears to be an attack coinciding with a Passover celebration parade. I don't have a count on the number of victims, but the casualty report indicates women, children, military and government personnel. These ordinances don't discriminate."

"What did *Voyeur* have on this?"

The secretary noted a pause before the reply.

"*Voyeur* had nothing, Frank. Just like Dublin...nothing at all. Between you and me, I have no idea what's going on, but I intend to find out."

"Jim, that's a concern... I have a concern. Certainly for the victims, but... you know what's at stake for the President—politically, I mean. Four years ago, he based his candidacy on *Voyeur*! Congress and the *U. N. Coalition* have invested *billions* of dollars in this program. With the reelection campaign heating up, I can only imagine what the opposition will do with this."

"I understand, Frank. We'll get to the bottom of this. Whatever it takes."

"Jim, we *must* get to the bottom of this—for everyone's sake. Where are we logistically?"

"I meet with the *chiefs of staff* in one hour. *Voyeur* has initiated Level 3 for the Middle East Sector. Reconnaissance and intelligence protocol are in place. I'll update you as soon as I can."

"Good! I'll call Dan Freeman at the White House and have him put me through to the President. He'll want to talk with us."

"I'll call you after the meeting."

* * * * * *

Tuesday, April 5, 2004
Atlanta, Georgia

As the metallic blue BMW coupe approached the gated security checkpoint, a laser beam scanned the front bumper of the German automobile for bar coded identification. Within milliseconds, a computerized system processed the information, prompting an electronic signal to open the gate.

Uninhibited, the vehicle passed through the guarded structure and onto the street. The advanced technology system was characteristic of upscale communities and a distinction among those with affluent lifestyles.

From the plush neighborhood, CNN Headline News anchor Jennifer Jones made a left turn onto Cherry Avenue. Glancing at the digital clock on dashboard, she noted the time—8:00 p.m. Jennifer was diligent about her work responsibilities and the preciseness of the schedule, though monotonous at times, ensured her punctuality.

Perfect! she thought.

Moving quickly, she traveled six blocks down the deserted street to the intersection of Interstate-285. At the freeway access ramp, Jennifer pressed the accelerator and the blue BMW responded effortlessly, blending seamlessly into the congested Atlanta evening traffic.

The Braves have a home game tonight...against the Mets, she thought as she finessed the German sports car along the highway. With contemplation, she glanced at the digital clock clustered among the LED lighted gauges of the dashboard.

"The game will be over in an hour. It won't be long before the

Turner Field crowd joins the Interstate evening parade."

If it wasn't the Braves, it was the Falcons, the Hawks, the Yellow Jackets...a concert...always something to make driving the Atlanta freeway an experience, especially at night! Giving the mental note little thought, she focused on her driving.

Moving fluidly with the flow of automobiles, Jennifer maintained a neutral position in the center lane of the highway. The ordeal of negotiating I-285 in heavy traffic was an experience with which she was by now keenly familiar.

Carefully, she monitored the traffic in the side and rear view mirrors. Comfortable with her position, she pushed the CD player selector located on the steering wheel and manipulated the volume control button with her right hand. Spontaneously, the voice of an Italian tenor emerged from the sound system as crisp, clear lyrics and harmonious notes filled the automobile with soothing music. The song was one of her favorites and listening to its melody relaxed her. It was a part of her mental preparation for an evening of work in front of the camera.

For the third time, she looked at the clock, noting the time. In fifteen minutes she would reach the Peachtree Street exit that would take her to downtown Atlanta and the CNN headquarters. She would park in the designated space reserved for her at the CNN employee garage.

Still on schedule, she exited I-285 and within minutes was approaching CNN. At Peachtree Street, she made a left turn in front of the building. At the parking garage entrance, the bar coded identification on the CNN bumper sticker of her BMW activated the laser scanner of the gate control. Jennifer paused briefly to allow the black and white striped gatepost to lift up and out of the passageway before proceeding, marveling at how technology could be both a blessing...and a curse.

The interior of the garage was well lit, making it easy to follow the driveway ramp to the assigned space. Bright, halogen lighting provided comfort as she locked her car and made the short walk to the elevator entrance of the headquarters.

Alone inside the elevator, the door closed as Jennifer spoke to the microphone on the control panel wall, "Fifth Floor." Immediately, the machine responded, moving smoothly up the shaft.

The fifth floor was the location of the main studio. Down its hallway were administrative offices, production studios and the dressing rooms for select CNN staff. Jennifer would begin her preparation for the evening telecast at her dressing room assigned to news anchor reporters.

At the designated stop, a soft bell-like tone sounded as the elevator door opened. There was no one in the hallway, but Jennifer smiled and waved to production room staff as she passed the large office windows of their workstations. Each person, no matter the size of their paycheck, was a part of the news team and among the best in their profession.

As she opened the hallway door to the dressing room suite, Jennifer noticed the production room assistant, Jack Wilson, leaning against the office doorway at the end of the corridor. Jack was dressed in gray slacks and a white dress shirt that was unbuttoned at the collar. A loosened, dark-striped tie completed his business attire.

Jack was in his mid-forties with balding dark brown hair. To cover the exposed scalp, he brushed the thinning hair from the side and across the top, left to right. Black, plastic "Roy Orbison" type frames accentuated the thick lens of the eyeglasses.

Overweight, Jack's stomach bulged against the buttons of his shirt, giving the casual observer good cause to believe that at any time the closures would pop and, quite possibly, do bodily harm. In his right hand was a clipboard jammed with papers. A ballpoint pen protruded from behind his left ear.

Appearing to be engaged in work, Wilson looked up from the notepad and smiled as she entered the hallway. Jennifer suspected that Wilson had the "hots" for her, although he had not crossed the line of sexual harassment. She could imagine the distorted fantasies running through his head.

The chance encounters with Wilson had happened before; too often to be coincidental.

Nevertheless, she knew how to handle it: Ignoring him was the only way to deal with his infatuation.

As she entered the dressing room suite, Jennifer greeted the staff that did her make-up, hair, and wardrobe. Mary Freeman, the staff assistant in charge, had worked with her for the past two years. Although they did not socialize outside of work, they were good friends who shared common interests in movies, shopping, and pets. Both owned a Jack Russell and loved to relate the never-ending stories about their energetic dogs.

The dressing and wardrobe suite was comprised of private rooms assigned to CNN reporters. A commons area provided space for final make-up and dress preparation. Other than wardrobe selection or perhaps a hairstyle change, the preparation routine was the same. Jennifer made small talk with the staff before moving to her private room to begin dressing.

"Good evening, folks," Jennifer greeted sincerely.

"Good evening, Jennifer," they replied in unison, their respect apparent.

"Mary, how's Tootsie?" she asked, referring to Mary's Jack Russell.

"Hey, what's the name of that song? Toot, Toot, Tootsie, Goodbye! I'm ready to kill her," Mary replied. "She was in my cross stitch bag this afternoon and pulled the thread box apart. I was not happy when I found her with her head inside the bag! When I scolded her, she looked at me with those innocent eyes like, 'Are you talking to me?' Sometimes I don't know what I'm going to do with her. Oh, she can be such a pain! But I love her."

"Hey, tell me about it. Spurrier has been his usual cantankerous self! He is so 'finicky' about his food."

Jennifer named her Jack Russell after the former University of Florida and her alma mater's football coach, Steve Spurrier. Their temperamental attitudes were a perfect match!

"If it's not the usual, he wants nothing to do with it. The vet's office was out of his brand the other day, and I picked up another. Boy, did he let me know about it! Whining... not eating. Finally, he got hungry enough to swallow what I had given him. What a pain! I know what you're talking about."

Similar small talk continued as the staff prepared Jennifer for her news shift. When the preparation was complete, she thanked the staff and walked from the suite, down the hallway, and into the studio. Along the way, she made a brief pit stop at the break room to fix a cup of hot tea.

Cup in hand, she walked to the studio and began the final briefing with the news staff. Within minutes Jennifer was "up to speed" on world events, which was the last phase of preparation before her scheduled newscast.

From the briefing, Jennifer learned that world news had been uneventful; nothing much was happening. Most likely, it appeared, she would spend the evening blending news stories of the day with entertainment, sports, and weather segments. Still, there was always the element of uncertainty when reporting world events. Sitting at the helm of breaking news offered an excitement that she craved.

Jennifer completed the briefing and noted the time on the studio clock: 9:50 p.m.

At 9:58 p.m., the newscast would go to commercial break, creating a transition for her news anchor stint.

Two minutes before the hour, CNN anchor John Shephard signed off. Looking across the studio, he smiled as he glanced at Jennifer standing in the background of the studio lights, behind one of the television cameras. The journalists were good friends who had been passing the anchor "baton" from one to another for more than a year.

Removing the lapel microphone from his tailored sports coat, John collected his paperwork and stood from the news desk chair. Looking again at Jennifer, he walked over to greet her.

"Hey, lady. How you doing?"

"Hi, John. Good! Looks as though things are routine. I can't believe the world is behaving itself for a change," she laughed.

"Yeah, other than the usual, not much happening."

Quickly, they exchanged well wishes and Jennifer moved to the anchor desk. With the exception of a short break each hour, she would occupy the anchor seat until 2:00 a.m.

* * * * * *

1:38 A.M., Thursday, April 6, 2004
CNN Studio, Atlanta

At 1:38 a.m. Jennifer was in the midst of completing the final thirty minutes of the late night CNN newscast. Staring at the lens of the studio camera, she dutifully read the script of a scrolling news story on the teleprompter screen. The routine was familiar; one she had been following for three and one-half hours now.

Throughout the evening, she reported headline stories, coupled with the usual blend of weather, sports, and entertainment news. The world had been quiet, for a change, almost too good to be true.

But the fleeting thought barely cleared her consciousness when it happened. The first indication was a flurry of activity in the wire news center at the back of the studio. With her peripheral vision, Jennifer detected the movement of several staff, including Program Director Bob Johnson. Bob was walking hurriedly to the wire news teletype desk.

Next was the cue from the lap top computer atop her news desk. On the screen, a blinking message typed in large font indicated an imminent, unscheduled, commercial break. Experience told her something was wrong; something dreadful, somewhere in the world, had gone wrong. Feeling the first leak of adrenaline bolt through her already alert system, Jennifer completed the news story and announced the commercial break.

Swiveling the chair at her news desk, she looked at the program director standing at the back of the studio. Bob returned her gaze and made a hand motion for her to come to him.

Quickly, a staff assistant approached the anchor desk and helped

Jennifer remove the lapel microphone from her suit. Standing from her chair, she walked to the back of the studio where Bob Johnson stood by the teletype; his face wore a colorless expression.

"Jennifer, apparently, there's been a terrorist attack in Tel Aviv. It sounds bad...civilian casualties and several top government officials!"

"The programmers are processing the script for the teleprompter. We've got Amanda Rappianne on the scene. Following your lead, we'll go to her. I didn't want you to be caught off guard. It doesn't sound good."

"Oh, God, Bob! I had a feeling...things were just too quiet. All those poor people. God! Do we know who did it?"

"Not yet. I'm sure we'll learn more from Amanda. It just happened. You ready?"

"I...I guess so."

Now, of course, there was little time to reflect. The broadcast would resume within minutes. Still, her heart was shattered to learn of another senseless tragedy.

When would it ever end?

* * * * * *

Tuesday, April 6, 2004
The Pentagon, Washington, D.C.

At 2:59 a.m., Joint Chiefs of Staff Chairman General James Wright, accompanied by several military staff assistants, negotiated the final security checkpoint of the inner sanctum of the Pentagon. At the end of the hallway, he entered the double doors of the Strategic Command Planning Room.

The windowless space was outfitted with state-of-the-art technology and served as the logistics post for global telecommunications, military operations, and national security. In the center of the room, executive-style chairs delineated the perimeter of an elongated semi-circular table. Each seat was comprised of a self-contained technology station. At designated locations, microphones defined the assigned placement of staff.

Surrounding the table, chairs, and technology stations were created work centers for military specialists and support staff. This morning members of the elite task force occupied every seat.

Nodding his head to acknowledge the assembly, the uniformed chairman walked to his leadership post at the end of the table. With his presence, the room immediately fell silent. Small talk faded quickly in transition to the business at hand.

Taking the seat, General Wright placed a black leather briefcase on the table. Manipulating the brass latches of the luggage with his hands, the locks "popped" twice as it opened, the sound only heightening the suspense now palpable in the otherwise silent room. From its contents, he removed a bundle of documents.

Spontaneously, a uniformed staff assistant, prompted by a gesture from the Chairman, moved to his side, took the stack of papers, and distributed them to the committee. As the chiefs and members of the staff scrutinized the report, the chairman spoke.

"Good morning, ladies, gentlemen. We have a problem. Let me repeat. *We...* have a problem. As you now know at approximately 9:00 a.m. Israel time an apparent terrorist bomb exploded in Tel Aviv. The significance of this occurrence is two-fold. First, the act of terrorism coincides with the celebration of a national holiday. Last month, Dublin—today, Tel Aviv.

"Secondly, there has been no advance intelligence—no warning, no recorded threats—nothing, absolutely nothing. At a time when the United States commands global reconnaissance systems capable of detecting a flea crawling up the ass of an elephant in Zimbabwe, we don't have the intelligence to intercept a terrorist strike on a parade of innocent citizens? I'm confident that you can appreciate the significance of this situation.

"We—the President, the people of the United States, the U.N. Coalition, you and I—have made a commitment to fight terrorism, both at home and abroad. *Voyeur* is the centerpiece of this united effort. Yet for all intents and purposes, the system has been dysfunctional. Unless you know something that I don't know, *Voyeur* simply has not worked!"

"Mr. Chairman, with all due respect, sir, how do we know it is capable of working in these situations? I mean... *Voyeur* may not be infallible."

Although Air Force General Robert Pierce presented the remark in a matter-of-fact, concerned manner, the statement nonetheless created a muffled stir among the assembly. Before General Wright could respond, others quietly echoed the comments.

The General continued, "How do we know the system is not flawed? How do we know if the system is capable of detecting these situations?"

"To speak candidly, sir, some believe that *Voyeur* was conceived as a political springboard for the administration and certain members of Congress. On the heels of the September 11th, 2001 attack in New

York, the American people and world leaders may have fallen victim to believe this system is foolproof—a safety net against the threat of terrorism. Until now the system had not been tested. How do we know with certainty that the system works? Personally, I'm not so sure."

Pausing to consider the question, General Wright responded with authority.

"General, ladies, gentlemen, you *are* correct. We do not know if the system failed. All of us recognize that man and his devices are not infallible. What we *do* know is the best and brightest minds in the world—dedicated engineers and military specialists—collaborated to make *Voyeur* the most advanced global intelligence gathering system in military history.

"We also know—and make no mistake about it—the President is committed to *Voyeur.* He expects us to use whatever means necessary to identify those responsible for these attacks. As for the politics, we leave that to the politicians. Our job is to assess where we are and what we need to do to correct or improve the system."

"The report that I have distributed is a confidential intelligence brief. It summarizes the events, as we know them. Every sector is at Recon Level 3. That is subject to change as circumstances develop.

"We will meet again today at noon. I expect a report from each sector commander. Review the protocol and database. Compile a summary and forward it to Vice Chairman Wood by 10:00 a.m. Contact me if necessary. Are there questions?"

There was no response from the group.

The orders were clear.

"We are dismissed."

* * * * * *

Tuesday, April 6, 2004, 7:00 A.M.
Atlanta, Georgia

CNN Headline News—Dateline: Tel Aviv, Israel, Tuesday, April 6, 2004:

"Good morning, I'm Carol Chaffey in Atlanta.

"This morning, in what ostensibly is the work of terrorists, a powerful bomb exploded in the midst of a Passover parade celebration. The death toll of Israeli citizens, government officials, and international visitors is yet-to-be determined, but officials say the number could exceed one hundred. Several NATO peacekeeping personnel, on duty in Tel Aviv, are reportedly among the victims. Ironically, the tragedy follows months of violence-free existence in the Middle Eastern city during which hope for peace in the unstable region have been at its highest in years.

"In Washington, the act of terrorism appears to have caught Pentagon and White House staff off-guard. For the second time in weeks, attacks coinciding with national holidays or religious celebrations have occurred without warning. Last month, in Dublin, Ireland, a similar bomb exploded in the midst of a Saint Patrick's Day parade. More than 100 Irish citizens, including children and government officials participating in the parade, were killed.

"Today, in an official statement, a U.S. government spokesman was uncertain as to who is responsible or how the acts of violence are being orchestrated. Ironically, both events occurred at a time when the United States and the United Nations' *International Coalition Against Terrorism* command the most advanced global anti-terrorist and homeland security system in the world: *Voyeur*.

"Earlier this morning General James Wright of the U.S. Joint Chiefs of Staff expressed confidence that the United States would identify those responsible for the attacks. Around the globe world leaders are expressing concern and condemnation of the tragic event.

"In Washington, breaking news of the Tel Aviv attack finds congressional leaders at a loss as to how to explain the tragedy. Four years ago, Congress extended extraordinary bipartisan support to President Stone and the global security system, *Voyeur*. Until now, the costly state-of-the-art technology had been untested.

"Now, in the wake of Dublin and Tel Aviv, members of Congress are rethinking their position. One senator, Richard Davis of California, is not at a loss for words; nor has he changed his opinion of *Voyeur*. For more on that story, we go to Washington *CNN* correspondent John Michaels... John."

"Good morning, Carol" the *CNN* reporter began as he took the lead.

"*Voyeur*, the world's most advanced global satellite surveillance and first-strike system ever conceived. Or is it?"

As the reporter spoke, the television screen displayed an animated version of a metallic-like satellite in space circling the earth. With each revolution, a series of pulsating red lines emanated from the spacecraft. Each pulsation simulated laser beams radiating downward from the satellite to the command center on earth.

With the next frame the animation expanded its scheme to create a matrix of satellites revolving in unison around the earth. The picture resembled a virtual web of sophisticated space technology that enveloped the earth like a blanket. On the global map, a blinking blue light represented the Central Command Post at the Pentagon. Deep within its confines, it housed a sophisticated technology mainframe capable of detecting virtually any means of communications on the planet.

"Touted as the ultimate global security system, *Voyeur* attracted support from across the international community. Without exception, members of the *United Nations' International Coalition Against*

Terrorism endorsed its deployment."

The television picture shifted to newsreel footage of the Capital and Congress in session, where Stone, the former senator from Ohio, was making a pitch for *Voyeur* before the legislative assembly.

"During his campaign for the presidency, Senator George Stone—now President Stone—led the *Voyeur* initiative. Stone's political prominence in Congress, coupled with strong bipartisan support, propelled *Voyeur* into space and his candidacy for President to the White House.

"But Stone's rise to political fame has not been without challenge. Four years ago, in a personally confrontational campaign for the highest office in the nation, Stone defeated hard-nosed California Senator Richard Davis. Throughout the campaign, Davis criticized Stone and his support for *Voyeur*.

"Following the defeat, Davis maintained his criticism of the President. With the reelection campaign heating up, his political animosity for Stone is not a secret.

"A few minutes ago, I spoke with the Senator as he arrived for a breakfast meeting of Congressional leaders. This is what he had to say about the developing events in Tel Aviv…"

The picture switched to a taped interview between the *CNN* reporter and Senator Davis conducted earlier at the steps of the Capitol building. Members of Congress and legislative staff arriving for the early morning meeting could be seen walking in the background. As the reporter extended the hand-held microphone in front of the senator, he began the interview.

"John, I don't want to be characterized as an 'I told you so' kind of guy, but *Voyeur* has failed. In the last two months, without warning, tragic events in Dublin and Tel Aviv have taken the lives of innocent men, women, and children; events for which the President led the United States and the *International Coalition* to believe *he* could handle.

"As a nation…in fact, as a global community, our security is no better today than it was four years ago. Billions of dollars have been invested…perhaps squandered…through this ineptness. The

President must be held accountable and the American people…people around the world deserve an explanation."

"Senator, your political feelings toward the President are no secret. Yet how can one individual—in this case, the President—be responsible for what has happened?"

"John, it's not about politics. More importantly, it is about leadership… about being forthright with the people. The system has failed us. It is not working! Homeland security and the war on terrorism is a shared responsibility between Congress and the administration. Both are accountable to the people. The President must address this issue. I can assure you that I will!"

"Thank you, Senator."

As the interview concluded, the live broadcast returned to the reporter.

"Carol, as you can see, the senator minces no words. He expressed harsh criticism of the administration and *Voyeur*. He was especially critical of the President and his homeland security plan. Over the next several weeks the Presidential election campaign will be interesting. Reporting from Washington, I'm John Michaels."

"Thank you, John," Carol replied, turning her attention back to the teleprompter.

* * * * * *

With one ring of the telephone, the voice answered.

"Frank?"

"Yes, Jim." The familiarity of the relationship between the secretary and chief-of-staff was by now well-established.

"Frank, I completed the initial briefing with the chiefs. Not much to report, other than what we discussed earlier this morning. We are reviewing the protocol for each *Voyeur* system and reconnaissance sector. Everyone has his assignment. We meet again at noon. I'll have more for you then."

"That's fine, Jim. I need to get what you have over to the President ASAP. I should be speaking with him at anytime."

"Yes, sir. I don't know what to think. It doesn't make sense."

"I know. We must get to the bottom of this. Call me when you have more. The President will want to talk with you."

"I'll be ready."

"For now, we'll handle the media together. Our position is that we are 'investigating the incident.' When we have something to share, we will... period."

"Thanks, Frank. I'll call you as soon as I can."

* * * * * *

The knock on the door was a formality, a gesture born of both military protocol and familiarity. Seated behind his desk, General Wright peered over the rim of his reading glasses and looked up. Standing before him was his Vice Chairman and colleague, Major General Douglas Wood. Concealing his inner stress, the Chairman mustered a look of determination as he greeted his friend.

"Yes, Douglas. Good morning."

"Good morning, General. I watched you at the meeting and I know *Voyeur* is bothering you. It bothers me...all of us. Whatever you need me to do...you just let me know."

"Thanks, Douglas. I don't know what the hell's going on. It doesn't make sense. We know the system is foolproof! The engineering...the tests...the research; it's proven...never been a problem...never!"

"And the people that worked on this project...the greatest minds in the world! Harry, Thomas, Wil—those guys are the best there is."

"I know, Douglas. We just have to stick with it. The communications staff is running the protocol. They should have something for us within the hour. Remember, whatever you need, you've got it. Something's got to turn up!"

"I believe that, too. We just have to figure out what."

Arranging the papers on his desk, the chief continued, "I'm supposed to meet with the secretary this morning. Until we know for certain what we're dealing with, I want to tighten the circle of information: The secretary and only those who *need to know*—you, me—will review the data. We don't know where this may go before it's over."

"Good. I'll follow up on the report and let you know."

"Thanks, Douglas."

The General turned toward the door to leave when the tone on the office intercom beeped. Pushing the speakerphone button, the chief responded, "Yes, Paula."

"I'm sorry to interrupt, sir, but it's the secretary's office on the line."

"Thank you, Paula," he replied, gesturing to the general, who was nearly out the door. "Douglas, I'll give you a call when I return from my meeting with the secretary."

"Yes, sir."

Turning his attention to the telephone call, he picked up the handset and spoke. "Yes?"

"General?" the voice on the other end of the line queried.

"Yes."

"Sir, please hold for the secretary."

Moments later, he heard the voice of the secretary of defense on the line. "Jim, good morning…again."

"Good morning, sir."

"The President wants to meet with us—you and me—in one hour. We'll ride together to the White House. You can brief me on the way. Meet me at my office in fifteen minutes. We'll go from there."

"Yes, sir. I still don't have much to give you. We are working on it. But I'll share what I have."

"Good. I'll see you in a few minutes."

* * * * * *

7:00 a.m., Tuesday, April 6, 2004
South Miami Beach, Florida

On any given spring morning in Miami, it doesn't take South Beach long to heat up. By daybreak the Florida humidity has a death-grip on any vestiges of the lingering, subtropical night. Most times it envelops you like a blanket—head to toe. For anyone, other than the natives, it's a nuisance—a headache that doesn't go away; something to complain about.

Locals call it their love-hate relationship with the environment—they *love* to *hate* it. Complain? Yes! But deep inside, they love it...they truly love it.

Frank Williams is a local. But he doesn't complain. And certainly not about a south Florida lifestyle he earned the old-fashioned way. After thirty years of distinguished service with the CIA, South Beach is his paradise. South Beach is his home. South Beach is his place to enjoy family and life. Humidity and all, he loves it.

Years ago, Frank and his wife, Peggy, purchased their south Florida dream home in a beautifully landscaped, subtropical section of South Beach. Minutes from Biscayne Bay and the Atlantic Ocean. Their years of meticulous care and attention enhanced its value many times over. Today, it's an upscale, eye-catching piece of what local developers love to call "prime real estate."

Throughout his career, Frank worked hard. From his fledgling start as a rookie agent, to retirement as director, Frank Williams worked hard. And, he was good, very good.

Frank was a family man and as a husband and father, he worked hard to fulfill his responsibilities. Now, he was working hard to be a good grandpa. The four-year-old grandson and two-month-old granddaughter his children had recently brought into the world are among the joys of his life.

Often, he and his loving wife, Peggy think "how nice it would be to have grandkids first!" Grandkids at a time when you could physically keep pace with their endless energy, that is! But then again, having lived a full life makes you appreciate the joy, love, and innocence they bring to life.

Every morning by 7:00 a.m., Frank is immersed in his daily routine—out of the bed at 6:00 a.m., twenty minutes of stretching and weights, a twenty-minute jog and twenty minutes in the pool swimming laps—a self-disciplined schedule he's followed for as long as he can remember. Now, his sixty-two-year-old body was addicted to a regimen that maintained his health and stamina.

Every day, following the morning exercise, instead of donning a business suit and heading to work, Frank enjoys a leisure breakfast on the swimming pool patio with Peggy: a cup of coffee, a glass of orange juice with time to peruse the headlines of the *Herald*.

"Goooood morning, Frank! Would you like some more orange?" Peggy asked breezily as she approached his refuge, fully expecting yet another "morning in paradise."

Frank, with his head immersed in the newspaper, did not reply.

"Frank, would you like some orange juice. Frank?"

"Uh, oh, uh, yes. Good morning, Peg. I'm sorry. Yes, I'll take some juice."

With a thick cotton terrycloth towel draped around his neck, Frank sat at the patio table by the pool. His eyes were riveted to the headlines of the *Herald*: "Terrorist Bomb Explodes in Tel Aviv!"

What in the hell is going on? he thought. *And just a month ago, Dublin...*

Immediately, his mind raced to his friend, General James Wright.

"I know Jim must be going crazy," he imagined. "Thank goodness I don't have to deal with *that* kind of stress anymore."

Still, after thirty years of service, the intrigue never leaves you. For a moment his mind wandered to his thirty years of career service.

Thirty years, he thought. *Twelve...fourteen hour work days, global travel, the separation from family and the stress—never knowing where the next event would take you. Sometimes it overwhelmed him...the responsibilities...the danger...the lives at stake...*

"Frank," Peg called. "What is it? What's on your mind this morning? You seem pretty interested in the *Herald*. That usually means only one thing: J-Lo must have a new movie out!"

"Tel Aviv got hit this morning."

"Tel Aviv?"

"Yeah. Apparently, a terrorist bomb exploded during the Passover celebration."

"What in the world? And things seemed to be settling down over there."

"I know. It doesn't make sense, but, you know, they never do."

"Were there casualties?"

"Apparently—according to the report—women, children, military personnel—a number of people."

"Oh, it's so sad. I just can't understand. Why? Frank, wasn't there something like this last month on Saint Patrick's Day in Dublin...a holiday parade... some kind of celebration?"

"Yes. I thought about the same thing—two national holidays in a row. Some coincidence, huh?"

"Terrible, so terrible!" Peggy sighed. "And those innocent people. *Why?*"

"I know, Peg. I know. I can't explain it."

Lost in their personal thoughts, there was a long pause before either one spoke.

"Frank, are we still planning to pick up the groceries and stuff for this weekend? Remember the kids are coming over."

"I'm ready when you are. As soon as we finish breakfast I'll get dressed. Are both of the kids going to make it?"

"As far as I know—that's the plan. I'll call them later to double check."

"Great! It will be fun."

Tuesday, April 6, 2004, 9:00 A.M.
The French Riviera, Southern France

Wilhelm Rulf grunted as his body tensed. From a prone position, lying motionless on the bed, he stared wide-eyed at the wall, listening intensely. Across the master bedroom of the French villa, the words of the *CNN Headline News* television report sent a familiar chill down his spine: "...terrorist...bomb...*Tel Aviv*..."

Keenly alert, a myriad of thoughts raced through his trained, self-disciplined frame of mind. Despite having retired from a bureau of *Interpol* in Germany two years previously, the stress-filled career as an international intelligence officer was not so easily abandoned.

From the bath shower, the soft Italian voice of his girlfriend Maria captured his attention.

"Wil... are you okay?"

"Yes, I'm fine."

Instinctively, he tried to make sense of the report. Flashbacks to past events reminded him of the ever-present threat of terrorism. Again, Maria's voice beckoned. This time, more pointedly.

"Wil, are you sure?"

Maria, Wil thought, *what a joy in my life.* He loved her intellect, her spirit...her charm. Not just beautiful, but a special friend. *His* companion. Despite an age difference of some thirty years, their relationship was filled with passion and romance.

At sixty, Wilhelm maintained the stamina and condition acquired during his younger, more athletic years. Daily workouts and running enhanced the physical appeal of his tall, rugged, masculine features—aquiline nose, dark hair, deep brown eyes, and broad chest. Women were immediately attracted to his good looks, no matter what their age.

"Yes, my love. It's the news report—a terrorist attack in *Tel Aviv*."

Maria was undaunted by the news. With a degree in telecommunications, graduate studies in political science, and five years experience as an intelligence specialist at the Zurich bureau of *Interpol*, she had forged a *hard-as-steel* attitude in dealing with international violence.

For the past month, in the wake of Dublin, her work had intensified. Every bureau was working around the clock to provide intelligence on the Saint Patrick's Day bombing to the CIA, *Voyeur*, and the Coalition. Now, with Tel Aviv, she could imagine the work that awaited her return to the Zurich office.

At times, the work overwhelmed her; the regime, endless. The rigorous routine made rendezvous with Wilhelm difficult, but somehow more…special.

For them, the French Riviera was a sabbatical—everything *Conde Nast Traveler* could describe—alluring, enchanting. It was easy to understand why worldwide travelers sought its romantic charm.

"They never seem to end…the attacks… the victims," she replied, walking into the bedroom from the bath as she toweled her hair dry. "There's something different here, though, given what happened last month in *Dublin*, and now, *Tel Aviv*."

"The United States will have a difficult time with this, especially the President. He put his career on the line with *Voyeur*. I wonder if they had any advance," she continued.

"From what you've told me about *Dublin*, I doubt it," Wilhelm responded.

Still, she wondered…

Clicking off the television remote control, Wilhelm changed the subject of the conversation. "Today, we go inland to the wineries," he exclaimed. "There are two vineyards we haven't visited. I want to try some of their Merlot. I hear it's exceptional!"

"I'm with you," Maria replied, walking across the room to kiss Wilhelm on the cheek. "Let's do it!"

* * * * * *

Tuesday, April 6, 2004, 8:00 A.M.
Oxford, England

You could always count on Harry. That's what Oxford political science professor Thomas Leed liked most about him. You could *always* count on Harry.

Every weekday, precisely at 8:00 a.m., Harry was there—tending his open-door coffee shop, sorting the magazines at his newsstand. By that time of morning, the curbside street location at *Harry's Newsstand* was a hub of activity—students, faculty, delivery trucks, and autos scurrying to predetermined destinations. Slowly, but surely, the university showed signs of life.

Thomas' early morning walk down cobblestone streets to the university was a routine he followed diligently. Depending on the weather, the professor dressed in a topcoat or sweater, scarf, and hat. A solid black umbrella, leather briefcase, and spectacles completed the attire that adorned his tall, lanky frame. *Harry's* was a brief stop, one block from the Oxford campus. The rendezvous always culminated in a short, but meaningful conversation between two friends.

Politics, current events, family; the topics varied according to circumstance or mood. Steaming cups of Colombian blend—no cream, no sugar—enhanced their time together. The early edition of the *London Times* "to go" was a given.

"Good morning, Harry," he said, extending his daily greeting.

Harry was of medium height, slightly overweight with graying hair, mustache, and wire rimmed glasses. This morning, as usual, he was wearing his traditional spring attire—light wool trousers, a white starched shirt buttoned at the collar, dark sweater, and full-length apron. A brown-leather touring style cap completed the wardrobe.

"Good morning, Professor. How's it going?"

"A bit cooler this morning, but nice. And you? How's Catherine?"

"Off to visit her sister," Harry replied, pouring the black coffee automatically. "The doctor gave her a good report yesterday. No sign of cancer anywhere. She's elated."

"How long has it been now, Harry?"

"Three years, Professor. Three years…a blessing!"

"The strides in medicine these days…amazing. That's great news!"

"Yes, 'tis. Not long ago it would have been tough for her." Sipping his coffee, Harry continued. "How are your classes? The semester's almost over, you know!"

"Excellent. Some of the best students; young, bright minds—always challenging my ideas… never agreeing. This generation—sometimes, I just don't know," he pretended to lament.

"Professor, I imagine you'll be talking about the headlines in the *Times* today!"

"Really?"

"Haven't you heard?" Harry queried. "The terrorist attack in Tel Aviv!"

"*Tel Aviv…Tel Aviv*," he inflected?

"This morning," Harry affirmed.

Tel Aviv, he thought, somewhat incredulously. The Middle East region had been quiet for some time. What could possibly be going on in *Tel Aviv*?

"Here," Harry said, extending a copy of the *Times* to the professor.

The professor's steel-blue eyes darted across the page, scanning the headlines: *Terrorists Attack Tel Aviv!—Passover Celebration Targeted.* The words leaped from the front-page story: innocent victims…bomb…no warning!

Quickly, his mind created an image of the event. A career in telecommunications as an intelligence officer with Interpol enabled him to relate to the news account. With ten years of service as Chief of the Interpol Bureau in London, Thomas recognized the significance of the news report.

"*Tel Aviv*," he pondered again...last month Dublin. The connection was immediate. "I wonder what *Voyeur* had on this?" he contemplated. "I'll bet James Wright is struggling with this right now."

James Wright, his life-long friend and colleague. They had shared years of government service together—James in the military, Thomas involved in telecommunications and international intelligence. Both distinguished themselves through courage, valor, and hard work.

Now, they maintained their friendship through regular correspondence and calls—sharing ideas, information; always supporting one another.

"Yes, I'm sure we will," the professor replied with distraction as his mind raced to distance itself from the present. "I'm sure we will."

The daily trek across campus from Harry's newsstand to the political science class in old Edward's Hall had transformed Professor Leed into a creature of habit. Every semester the professor negotiated the familiar routine countless times on his way to and from class. By the end of the term, every step, sidewalk, door, and stairway was practically automatic.

This morning the news of Tel Aviv preoccupied his mind. Fortunately, the repetition of the morning ritual kept him on track. As he approached the classic red brick structure of Edward's Hall, the shout of a female voice captured his attention.

"Professor Leed! Professor Leed!"

Turning in the direction of the sound, his eyes settled on the familiar young face of his graduate assistant, Elizabeth Stall.

"Good morning, Elizabeth," he replied.

"Good morning, Professor. Have you heard the news?"

"And what news might that be," the professor replied knowingly, ever the teacher. Elizabeth's keen mind and unquenchable thirst for international politics never missed breaking news of current events.

"Tel Aviv!" she exclaimed, confirming his intuition. "Tel Aviv! There was a terrorist attack this morning in Tel Aviv, a bomb of some sort! Reports say there are many casualties; much like what happened last month in Ireland."

"Yes. That's what I understand. I was just down at *Harry's*. He gave me a copy of the *Times*. It made the headlines." His irony was lost on her.

"And what do *you* make of this?" the professor queried the young scholar.

"I don't know, sir. I just don't know. Two attacks in the last two months—both on national holidays. Some coincidence, don't you think?"

"Yes. I must agree it's a coincidence...if nothing else. I'm sure it will be a topic for discussion in class today."

"Yes, sir, professor. I'm on my way to pick up the 'stat' report on the data we ran yesterday...if that's okay with you? They said it would be ready first thing this morning. I was going to bring it to your office before class."

"Yes, that will be fine. I'm on my way to the office and then to class. I'll see you shortly."

"Yes, sir. I'll see you soon."

* * * * * *

Primitive by 21st Century standards, the Morse code signal navigated the short wave frequency like a Magellan explorer. Then, milliseconds later, vanished into radio space:

Money transfer complete.... Will make contact after Cinco de Mayo.... Happy Holidays ....

* * * * * *

Secretary Frank Baker and General James Wright walked shoulder to shoulder down the corridor of the Pentagon through the security checkpoint to the building exit. Two staff assistants carrying briefcases followed several feet behind the two officials.

With each step, the sound of their leather soles against the tile floor reverberated against the walls of long corridor; the echo muted the idleness of their conversation. They would wait for the sanctum of the staff limousine parked outside to discuss the highly classified information.

Moments later, the two men were passengers inside the black automobile with white government license plates, speeding toward Pennsylvania Avenue. At the White House, the President awaited their arrival.

Despite the congestion of the business-day traffic, the sleek vehicle moved smoothly along an oft-traveled route. The spring morning at the nation's capital was clear and crisp. They traveled less than a block from the Pentagon when the Secretary began the conversation. "Jim, I know it's early in the investigation, but the President is expecting answers. He feels the pressure."

"I know, Frank. But we've checked everything—every system, every protocol, the whole routine—everything! I don't know. Right now, I just don't know!"

"For the time being, then we'll stick to what we do know—what happened in Tel Aviv—the ordinance, the casualties, the protocol…all of that. We'll deal with the '*why*' part later. I don't know if that will satisfy him, but it's all we have. You present the Tel Aviv report, I'll deal with the system issues…*and* the politics."

"Yes, sir," the general replied.

* * * * * *

Tuesday, April 6, 2004
Meeting with the President - The White House

The uniformed armed services guard snapped to attention and saluted as the black limousine approached the gated checkpoint. Military protocol was an integral part of White House security procedures.

As the vehicle slowed to a stop, the limousine driver activated the electronic window lock and handed a packet of credentials to the checkpoint officer. Taking the packet from the driver, the soldier scrutinized the passengers as he studied the credentials. Turning his back to the automobile, he passed the identification papers to a second guard inside the checkpoint station for processing. Moments later, the officer signaled their clearance, returned the credentials and saluted again. It was a procedure that was repeated countless times every day. In the aftermath of *9/11*, nothing was taken for granted.

Proceeding, along the driveway the limousine moved to a secluded compound at the rear of the White House. There another uniformed guard saluted the occupants as the limousine moved to its designated parking space.

Immediately, two uniformed officers approached the vehicle and opened the passenger door for its occupants. The Secretary and General offered cursory salutes of protocol as they stepped from the car.

From the automobile, they walked quickly to the rear entrance of the White House. At the doorway, a security screening station was located adjacent to the elevator. One by one, they stood in front of the sensor to activate the screening process. Within seconds, the sophisticated identification system performed an iris scan, fingerprint comparison and DNA analysis. A blinking green light on the control panel signaled their clearance for entry into the headquarters of the President.

Stepping away from the checkpoint, the officials entered the open elevator entrance and waited quietly for the doors to close. There was no conversation among the group.

Moments later, the elevator reached its destination and access to the inner sanctum of the President. When the door opened, Dan Freeman, the President's chief of staff, greeted them.

"Good morning, gentlemen, the President is expecting you. How are you doing, James…Frank?"

"Don't ask," the secretary replied.

"That bad," Freeman replied.

"That bad," the secretary responded as the group of officials made their way down the hallway to the Oval Office.

Original oil paintings of historical significance adorned the ornate walls of the corridor. No matter how many visits he made to the Oval Office, James Wright always felt goose bumps when he was inside the workplace of the President of the United States. This morning those emotions were heightened even more as he thought about the significance of his meeting with the President.

Taking the lead, the chief of staff entered the spacious office, followed by the

Secretary and the General. The President, seated at his desk, looked up from his work.

Standing, he extended his hand in greeting to the three men.

"Good morning, gentlemen—Dan, Mr. Secretary, General."

"Good morning, Mr. President," they responded individually.

"We have coffee, juice, pastries…whatever you like," the President offered, gesturing to the neatly anointed silver trays on the coffee table.

"Coffee for me," the secretary responded.

"Make that two," echoed the general.

"Three," Dan Freeman grinned.

Taking a moment to prepare their beverage, the men took seats around the table. A quiet knock on the doorway shifted their attention as Secretary of State William Thomas entered the room.

"Mr. Secretary," the President acknowledged. "Good morning."

"Good morning, Mr. President, Dan...Secretary...General."

"Good morning," they replied in unison.

"Bill, help yourself to some coffee," the President offered. "There's juice and pastries, too."

"Thank you, sir. Coffee will be fine."

When everyone was seated, the President began the meeting.

"Gentlemen, what do we have? What the hell's going on in Tel Aviv'?"

"Mr. President," Secretary of Defense Franklin Baker began. "If I told you more than 'I don't know,' I would mislead you. I know you don't want that."

"At the same time, I can tell you that we—the general and I—are doing everything possible to get to the bottom of this."

"Mr. President," the general continued, "we are as puzzled as you—as anyone in this room—as to why *Voyeur* hasn't given us the reconnaissance we expected it to give. Thus far, every system checks out—every protocol, every sector. We just don't know.... But I promise you, we will!"

"Gentlemen," the President responded. "You know the pressure we are under. State leaders around the world are calling. Congress is showing signs of agitation. Before long the damned politics will begin... You know the drill.

"But what I don't understand is the system...*Voyeur,*" the President continued. Do we have a problem? I need to know. Good or bad, I need to know!"

"Sir," the general responded. I don't think we can say... not at this point. Perhaps, but I don't think so. There's been too much vested in its development. Give me time and we will get to the bottom of this."

"We don't have time," Dan Freeman retorted forcefully, standing from his chair! We need answers... *now!"*

"Dan's right, Mr. President," Secretary Thomas added with a tone of irritation. We're getting calls. People want answers...now!"

"So what do you suggest we do differently," Secretary Baker challenged. "Don't you understand we are doing everything we know to do? We're conducting a thorough check of every protocol, every system, everything!"

"Well, whatever the hell it is, it's not enough," Freeman countered!

"Gentlemen," the President intervened.

"Mr. President," Dan Freeman, responded. "With all due respect, sir. We need answers and it's their job to find them! This will be tough on you... especially with the campaign...the politics. It's going to get messy!"

"I understand, Dan. We are all under stress—pressure is everywhere! Yes, we need to figure this out. Yes, we need answers. But we must do so with a sense of purpose. Bickering gets us nowhere!"

"James...Frank," the President continued, "I have confidence in you. I trust you. I also have confidence in *Voyeur*. We've invested too much. We've researched the system. It should work *for* us, not against! The challenge...our challenge is to figure this out."

Without pausing, the President directed.

"Continue your efforts at the Pentagon. Keep the circle of information tight and under control. Keep me posted. Whatever you learn, I need to know. Frank and I will handle the politics, the Congress and the heads of state."

"Dan, get with Cindy and arrange a press conference for later this morning. We'll give it to them straight. Let them know we are working on it. We *will* get to the bottom of this! Does anyone have a question?"

The President stood from his chair to indicate the meeting was adjourned.

"No, sir," they replied in unison.

"Thank you," the President offered, as he turned to the paperwork on his desk. "I expect to hear from you."

HAPPY HOLIDAYS: A POLITICAL THRILLER

* * * * * *

The staff driver maneuvered the black limousine deftly through the morning traffic and across the Potomac, retracing its route back to the Pentagon. From the rear seat, James Wright daydreamed as he stared out the passenger window. The hypnotic, streaming frames of the Washington landscape created a kaleidoscope of color in his mind. Cast against the distorted backdrop, businessmen and women, pedestrians and tourists, performed their daily exercise of life in a big city.

But that routine had changed—nothing like it used to be. *9/11* had taken care of that. Now, throughout the city, areas with limited public access were common. Security checkpoints and uniformed guards at prominent locations were readily visible. And public tours to historical landmarks like the Pentagon were restricted. It was not the same.

Yet there was little that people could know, much less understand, about developing world events. It was at these times that James Wright realized the significance of his role to the destiny of a nation and how humbling that role could be.

"Last month, Dublin, today, Tel Aviv. What next?" He didn't want to think about it. Not now, at least. His brain was on overload—too many questions…too few answers. Who was involved? Why hadn't *Voyeur* detected the communication plan? What was the motive?

The meeting with the President was as he had expected. Not as he had hoped, but what he expected—predictable. You could cut the tension with a knife—finger pointing, insinuations.

Who the hell does Dan Freeman think he is, anyway? If he can do something we haven't done, let him! Damn! We've worked our tails off since 2:00 a.m., he thought. *Wait, just wait! When we figure this out, he can kiss my ass! I've had it with his political bullshit!*

Fifteen minutes, he thought, looking at his watch. *We'll be back at the office…at the Pentagon. Woods… I need to see Woods; see if he's come up with anything. Hopefully, he has something to go on.*

Things to do…staff briefing, review system protocols, prepare for the chief's meeting...what else?

It doesn't make sense. This whole thing doesn't make sense. The guys who designed this system are the best! There's got to be an explanation...

What am I saying? What am I saying? There is an explanation! I've just got to find it!

Susan. I've got to call Susan. Surely, she's heard by now. What a way to ruin her trip. She'll be worried. She always worries—about me; about my work. I couldn't do it without her.

"Jim...Jim!" the voice of the secretary resounded in his mind like an alarm. Now aware of his surroundings, he recognized the voice of his boss, seated across from him in the limousine.

"How long was I out?" he asked, referring to his daydream.

"For just a few minutes. Actually, I was doing the same thing. You know...trying to figure this thing out."

"Jim, do you think we have a conspiracy on our hands," the secretary queried.

"Conspiracy?"

"Yes, a conspiracy...someone with a plan...make *Voyeur* fail. Someone with a motive."

"*Conspiracy.* I think it's *possible*. I haven't ruled anything out at this point. We really know very little right now. We're following the system protocol...the usual. I haven't focused on a conspiracy theory. Is there something you know?"

"No, not really—a hunch maybe, or just a thought. Keep it in mind, though...and cover your ass!"

From the back seat of the limousine, James Wright gazed at the Pentagon looming in the distance. Despite its familiarity and the hours he spent there, the massive structure overwhelmed him. Looking at the historical landmark was a timeless experience—like watching a NASA shuttle launch or Tiger Woods hit a tee shot—it was simply an awesome sight.

Comprised of three times the floor space of the Empire State Building, the Pentagon provides workspace for more than 23,000 employees. Seventeen and a half miles of corridors and 100,000 miles of telephone cable create a world-class infrastructure for telecommunications, technology, and information processing.

But the heart and soul of the Pentagon is its people—the military workforce and staff. Collectively, they are a proud, unflappable group of American workers who take pride in public service. Led by a popular secretary of defense and chief of staff, their spirit is woven like fabric by the steel-like threads of *9/11*.

At the parking garage, the general cleared the security checkpoint where he took the elevator to the floor of his office. As he entered the compound, James felt the undeniable tension emanating from Pentagon staff passing along the corridor. Tel Aviv had exposed everyone to the increased pressure of world events. Salutes of protocol were transparent veils from which contorted faces of anxiety appeared.

Turning the hallway corner, James approached the headquarters of his Pentagon office. Inside the doorway was the reception area. In this room, distinctive furniture and the prominent seal of the office in the center of the back wall depicted an image of great responsibility. Near the doorway, seated behind her desk, was his secretary Paula Spencer.

Paula was a veteran civil service employee whose lifelong career in public service spanned the administration of several chiefs of staff.

Although Paula and the general were not long-time acquaintances, her work ethic and intellect quickly earned his respect. Coupled with a warm personality and unqualified commitment to her work, she became a confident in which placed his greatest trust.

Professionally, they worked as a team, taking on the many challenges of the job. But their friendship never overlooked the opportunity to share family experiences and personal interests. It was this dimension of the relationship that kept the stress of work in perspective.

Paula admired the general for his integrity and leadership. He was her respected boss; a friend she could depend on.

Now, she was concerned about his well-being. Through her experience she understood the pressure he was under and would do everything possible to help him deal with its uncertainties.

Looking up from her desk, she acknowledged his presence with a smile. "Good morning, General. How was the meeting with the President?"

"Is that a loaded question? As if you didn't know." His smiling expression was obviously fabricated.

Chuckling, she replied. "No, let me guess…uh…*Dan Foresman?*"

"You said that. I didn't," the general quipped.

"You didn't have to. His finger pointing is written all over your face! Did he give you any suggestions on how much better *he* could have handled this situation?"

"Paula, your intuition scares me. You and Susan think too much alike. I don't stand a chance…at home *or* at work."

"Hey! You guys are all alike. Frank is the same way at home. I can read him a mile away!" She laughed. "Speaking of Susan, Mrs. Wright just called. She asked that you call her… at her sister's. She's worried. We all are…I have the number."

"I expected she would call. I was about to call her. As for the '*worrying about me,*' that's *not* in your job description. Keep it up and I may have to write you up in your evaluation," he joked.

"Hey! Write me up, if that's the way you feel! I'm a big girl. I can take it!"

"*Okay*, have it your way."

Walking to his office door, he turned to look at Paula.

"I'm going to call her. You have the number?"

"Yes," she replied, holding the telephone message slip in her hand.

Walking toward her, he took the message slip.

"Would you contact General Wood's office? Ask if he could meet with me in about fifteen minutes. I want to brief him on my discussion with the President. And we need to prepare for the noon meeting with the chiefs."

"Yes, sir."

Walking into his office, the general took a seat in the executive style leather chair at his desk. The spacious work center, located near a large floor-to-ceiling window, offered a panoramic view of the Potomac and the city.

The desk and furniture were distinctive. Solid cherry, polished to a high-gloss finish. A telephone, intercom, fountain pen holder and brass nameplate anointed the desktop. To the side, a computer, printer, and fax machine provided technology support. The *In Box* on the corner of the desk was stacked with mail. *That*, he thought, *would have to wait.*

Lifting the handset of the telephone from its cradle, he read the telephone message slip and punched the touch-tone numbers. Spontaneously, the telephone at his sister's home began to ring.

He swiveled his chair to face the window. With his back to the desk, the panoramic view of the distant Washington cityscape momentarily refreshed him. Within moments, a familiar voice answered the call.

"Hello?"

"Anne?" It was Susan's sister.

"James! How are you? Susan was expecting your call. It's all over the news...she's worried about you."

"I'm fine. Another day in the life...as they say."

"James, you *know* Susan always worries about you, regardless of how many times you deal with these crises. Hold on, let me get her."

"Thanks. I worry about her, too."

Within moments, Susan was on the line.

"James, I've been watching the news. I'm worried."

"I'm fine. I was going to give you a call. I just returned from a meeting with the President and secretary. We have a full day ahead of us. What are you and Anne up to? How's the visit going?"

"Oh, we've had a great time. We took the kids to the zoo, the movies and, *of course*, found a *little* time for shopping. They have a new mall not far from here and we had to *'check it out'!*"

"Exactly. You wouldn't want to miss out on an opportunity like that," he teased. "It's good talking with you, *Love*. You know I miss you. It's going to be pretty busy for a while."

"I understand. I miss you, too! I'll be here until the weekend. I'll give you a call before then. You call me, too! You hear?"

"I hear. You know I will. Give my regards to everyone. I'll keep you posted...love you!"

"I love you, too. Bye."

James Wright placed the telephone handset on it cradle and turned his attention to the paperwork that had accumulated on his desk. Despite the best use of technology it was impossible to abandon the "old fashioned way" of communicating on paper. Chuckling, he thought of the "efficiency experts" and their endless pursuit to eliminate government paperwork.

"Good luck!! I can tell you right now that *ain't* happening. At least not in *my* lifetime!"

Sorting through the memoranda and department bulletins, his mind drifted to Tel Aviv. What he could not understand was how it had happened without advance intelligence? Somehow... someway, he had to get to the bottom of it.

Deep in his thoughts, the sound of the intercom on his desk startled him. "General?" It was the voice of his secretary Paula. "General Wood is here. Do you want me to have him come in?"

"Yes, Paula. That will be fine."

A brief knock on the door preempted the entrance of the General.

"Good morning again, James."

"Good morning, Jim."

"Coffee?"

"No, I'm good for now. How did it go with the President?"

"That's what I wanted to talk with you about. Predictable. Dan Forsman and his attitude—he can always do things a little better than you and I. He may be good at what he does, but he has an attitude like the rear end of a mule"

"You got that right. How is the President taking this? What does he want us to do?"

"He continues to amaze me. He is really steady...and I know he feels the pressure. Hell, we *all* are!"

"He affirmed his confidence in what we are doing ... said he would take care of the politics and for us to do our job—what we know best to do. He wants us to keep him informed with the progress. You can't ask for more than that."

"Jim, we still don't have anything new. I ran the protocol on every system. Nothing has turned up. I told the staff to run them again. There's got to be something we haven't picked up."

"Good. I'll prepare an agenda for the meeting with the Chiefs. I'll set up a schedule for the system check and reporting. We have to stay with it until something turns up."

"Yes, sir. I'll have my report ready ... Noon, right?"

"Yes, that's what we said."

Turning to leave, the general replied, "Good. I'll see you in a little bit."

"Douglas, just one more thing before you go."

"Yes, sir?"

"Douglas, do you think it's possible we are dealing with a conspiracy?"

"*Conspiracy?*"

"Yes, conspiracy. Something that is disrupting *Voyeur*."

"Well, I think it's too soon to rule *anything* out at this point. To tell you the truth, it has not crossed my mind. What makes you think there may be a conspiracy?"

"Nothing, really. Just this morning…on the way back to the Pentagon from our meeting with the President…the secretary asked me the same thing. It caught me off guard."

"I can understand. What did you say?"

"Pretty much what you did. I don't think we can rule out anything, but it's too soon to jump to conclusions. Running the protocols and system check is complicated. It will take time."

"You've got that right! We've got our hands full! I'll keep my eyes open. If you want me to do anything, let me know."

"No, just a thought—something that was mentioned. We've got a lot more work to do first."

"I'll see you at the meeting."

"Good."

* * * * * *

The "*On the Air*" studio cue light switched from red to green as the taped commercial ended its time segment. *CNN Morning Headline News* hostess Lynn Gabriel, wearing a red suit trimmed with a black collar, glanced at the television monitor, looked directly at the camera lens, and began her opening dialogue with confidence and precision.

"Good morning, I'm Lynn Gabriel from Atlanta and this is the *Morning News*.

"Today's top story is an apparent terrorist bombing in Tel Aviv. This morning, at approximately 9:00 a.m. in Tel Aviv, a powerful bomb exploded amidst a *Passover* parade celebration. Scores of men, women and children, including several top Israeli government officials, were killed. Still unexplained is the motive and those responsible for this act of violence. Reporting live from Tel Aviv is Amanda Rappianne."

The television image changed to a street scene of destruction and devastation. Emergency vehicles, medical personnel, and citizens plundered through the rubble searching for victims and the wounded. The chaotic picture created a backdrop as *CNN* field reporter Amanda Rappianne presented her report.

The reporter was dressed in black slacks, a magenta-blue blouse, and a black leather jacket. A light breeze tossed her dark, shoulder-length hair as she pressed the audio monitor against her right ear with her hand. Taped video footage of the Passover parade, taken moments before the powerful explosion ripped through the assembly, rolled across the screen. Holding the microphone with her left hand she moved it close to her mouth to reduce the distraction of background noise.

"Good morning, Lynn. As you see, Tel Aviv is reeling from the impact of an apparent terrorist bombing. Earlier this morning, without warning, a sophisticated bomb, seemingly placed strategically along the Passover Parade route, exploded, killing scores of Israeli citizens, military personnel and government officials. The powerful blast leveled the street for more than a block, setting fire to countless buildings and vehicles at 'ground zero.'

"As we survey the devastation, rescue workers and volunteers continue their search for victims and the missing. Obviously, it will be some time before an estimate of casualties and wounded can be made. It's a terrible scene that some describe as 'One of the nation's worst tragedies in recent times'. "

"Amanda, what are officials saying about those responsible for the attack?"

"Lynn, right now the focus is on rescue and medical attention for the wounded. Officials tell me they have no leads or suspects—no expressed motive. And no group or organization has come forward to accept responsibility.

"As you know, Tel Aviv is the center of a politically unsettled region which, historically, has been vulnerable to attack. Still, the destruction contains all the signs of organized terrorism."

"Thank you, Amanda. It certainly is a tragedy and we look forward to your next report."

Turning her attention to the studio camera, the *CNN* anchor continued the *Morning News* broadcast: "Two international terrorist bombings in two months; both coinciding with national holiday celebrations. Coincidence or circumstance? And why was there no warning? After all, the international community has invested billions of dollars in *Voyeur* to give advance warning of terrorist threats.

"Joining us today in the studio to address these questions is retired Major General Robert Dempsey. General Dempsey is a decorated army intelligence officer and military consultant for the United States Department of Defense. Before his retirement, he played a key role in the development of the technologically integrated, global intelligence network, *Voyeur*. His understanding of the system and its capability is unsurpassed.

"Good morning, General, and thanks for being with us today."

The picture switched from the reporter to a stage set where General Dempsey stood before a multi-colored mural map of the world. A graphic overlay, outlined in red, depicted the satellite reconnaissance network, *Voyeur*.

Dressed in a dark business suit, white shirt, and striped tie, the general held a metal, rod-like pointer in his hands. Neatly trimmed gray hair and sharp facial features enhanced his look of distinction and authoritative role.

"Thank you, Lynn. It's my pleasure."

"General, let's begin by discussing the two incidents...last month, Dublin, today, Tel Aviv. Both attacks occurred during holiday celebrations. A connection, or purely circumstance?"

"Lynn, no one can say with absolute certainty at this point. Despite *Voyeur*, intelligence gathering remains a challenge. What we *know* is the attacks occurred on national holidays and involved similar types of ordinances; *those factors* need to be considered."

"General, both attacks came without warning. Yet when President Stone and the Department of Defense introduced Voyeur, the system was touted as 'fool-proof'; a major selling point that convinced the United Nations and members of the international community to 'buy in' to the program. What has happened?"

"*Lynn, as far as Voyeur* is concerned, we don't know that anything has happened. It will take time to answer that question. What we must do—the United States and the *U.N. Coalition*—is to review security protocols, analyze every system—*everything...every component*, must be checked and rechecked. Then, and only then, can we draw conclusions. In the meantime, I imagine that Chief of Staff General Wright**,** and the department are doing that very thing—most likely as we speak!"

"General, at the time of its development, you were involved in the system design for *Voyeur*. Explain, if you will, how *Voyeur* works and what distinguishes it from other, let's say...'*Traditional*' reconnaissance systems. What makes *Voyeur...foolproof?*"

"Lynn, I don't know anyone knowledgeable, who was involved in the development of *Voyeur*, that would describe the system as absolutely *foolproof.* State-of-the-art? Yes. The best system ever? Absolutely! Beyond that, mankind and his devices are far from perfect.

"What we have, Lynn, is a global surveillance system designed by the best and brightest minds on the planet—intelligence officers, scientists, military experts, system analysts around the world collaborated on this project.

"Is it perfect? No. Is it the best we can imagine or hope for? I think so."

"What, then, General, distinguishes *Voyeur* from intelligence gathering systems of the past?"

"Lynn, in many of its components, *Voyeur* employs traditional satellite and intelligence gathering technologies. It has the capability of initiating a first-strike or defense response anywhere on the planet.

"In other words, if the Coalition is attacked, or is even in imminent danger of attack, *Voyeur* provides the intelligence to preempt or respond to that threat?"

"Yes, and the response can be targeted, specific, preemptive or defensive, depending upon the circumstances of the perceived threat."

"What, then, distinguishes *Voyeur* from other systems?"

"Its distinction, Lynn, and what separates *Voyeur* from all others, is its language encryption system."

"Language encryption? That sounds interesting."

"Lynn, not only is it interesting, it is truly a work of intelligence gathering genius.

"In the development of *Voyeur*, language specialists—experts in their field—from around the world created an extraordinary language data base in the *Voyeur* mainframe. But that alone is not what distinguishes the system.

"The uniqueness is the nature of the data base—key words, phrases, codes—even specific messages—encrypted in *every known language and dialect in the world.* Each language '*chunk,*' through its interpretation and meaning within the context of acts of violence—terrorism if you will—raises a "red flag" in the *Voyeur* system.

"Once detected, *Voyeur* pinpoints the source and its location within a matter of seconds. The system is so advanced, its precision can provide critical information and most importantly, time for a preemptive response."

"But, General, isn't what you describe basically 'Big Brother'?

How can the people of the world expect any level of privacy with a global eaves-dropping system that monitors every word, message or communiqué? Are there not legal issues involved with a system like this?"

"Lynn, you are absolutely correct. Initially, there were concerns. But again, *Voyeur* is a sophisticated system with remarkable discretion. Unless it detects a specific sequence of pre-programmed words and phrases, *Voyeur* ignores the transmission. Countless tests and close scrutiny from the international community have convinced critics of its extraordinary capability."

"In other words, General, combinations of common words and every day phrases, regardless of language or point of origin, do not activate the alert system?"

"Exactly."

"What then, General, would keep, let's say, terrorists from mimicking unobtrusive language in their transmissions?"

"Lynn, that's an excellent question. Messages—words, phrases— have a nature about them; a context within which they are relayed. *Voyeur* makes that distinction. Furthermore, the system is continually updated and revised, responding to changes in language and clandestine codification as they occur."

"General, this is extraordinary—truly unheard of."

"Yes, it is."

"Before we conclude, General, how then, if *Voyeur* is all we believe it to be, have terrorist operatives and their messages gone undetected?"

"Lynn, I don't know. Time must answer that question for us."

"Thank you, General, I'm sure we will talk with you again as these events unfold."

"Thank you, Lynn. It's my pleasure."

* * * * * *

Tuesday, April 6, 2004
West Wing - The White House

The history of the West Wing of the White House dates to the first full-term of President Thomas Jefferson. During this period, Jefferson proposed one-story extensions to the east and west to connect the President's house with adjacent office buildings. The terraces that connect the residence of the White House with the East and West Wings were among the design concepts President Jefferson envisioned.

Although the terraces were used for household functions, they did not provide additional office space. And, for the remainder of the century, through the administrations of Harrison, Cleveland, and McKinley the executive offices took up much of the second floor of the residence. In 1902, President Theodore Roosevelt moved the presidential offices from the residence to the addition that became known as the West Wing.

Today, the West Wing houses the Presidential Oval Office, the offices of his executive staff, the Cabinet Room, the Roosevelt Room, and the James S. Brady Press Briefing Room. It was from the front of the Brady Room that White House Press Secretary Cindy Johnson stood poised and confident behind a podium clustered with microphones.

Surveying the "standing room only" audience with her eyes, she recognized familiar faces framed within the array of television cameras, photographers, and technical assistants. Catching her gaze, they smiled at her in recognition.

Many were long-time friends or colleagues; others, political rivals, armed with their agenda. Each knew the protocol and would assume their respective roles. The press briefing had become an important element in the process of a democratic government.

The room, though plainly anointed, served its purpose. Within its four walls, political events were debated, presidential decisions questioned and press secretaries grilled. Today would be no different.

But for Cindy Johnson, it was a moment that she relished; the opportunity to test her fortitude under fire. Candid and honest, she had the uncanny ability to perform under pressure; a quality her colleagues revered.

Cindy possessed a keen intellect and charismatic personality. Coupling these traits with a strong work ethic had obviously served her well. Nothing, absolutely nothing, rattled her; the more difficult the situation, the better. She was *"Old School."* As a professional, Cindy worked hard to establish her career. Numerous awards for journalistic merit preceded the national prominence of press secretary to the president.

Cindy glanced at her wristwatch, noting the time. It was 1:00 p.m. Looking to the back of the room, she responded to the cue from a technician standing by a monitor. Without hesitation, she began to speak.

Spontaneously, cameras flashed and camcorder motors whirred. There was no anxiety in her voice. "Good afternoon. Let me give you a report on the President's day and the week ahead. This morning the President held his usual round of briefings, followed by meetings with key members of his national security staff.

"Later, in a televised broadcast, the President addressed recent events in the Middle East and the tragic bombing in Tel Aviv. In his report, the President indicated that little is known about those involved or the motivation behind the despicable attack. The President was clear in his resolve to bring those responsible to justice.

"Every system, every department, and every available resource has been dedicated to this initiative. As more information is obtained, it will be reported.

"Later today, the President will make remarks on American Education Month in the East Room, then depart the White House for Camp David where he will hold a series of scheduled meetings and work. With that opening statement, I'll take your questions."

Quickly, she recognized Bob Reneger, a veteran AP journalist sitting near the front of the assembly.

"Yes, Bob?" she queried.

"Is *Voyeur* a failure?" he asked bluntly.

Using her quick wit, she responded. "Thanks, Bob. I knew I could count on you for a tactful *icebreaker.* Let's dispense with the formalities and get to the heart of the matter!"

A quiet chuckle moved through the room.

"Bob, right now, you and I don't have all the answers. Neither does the President. He made that perfectly clear in his remarks this morning. What we do know is his commitment to use every available resource to combat these attacks.

"As for *Voyeur*, every test and every study has supported its reliability. At this point, there is no basis to question its reliability. If, for any reason...*any* reason, the President doubts its capabilities, I assure you, he will be the first to confront it."

"But still, Cindy," Bob asked in redirect, "you know as well as I that many say *Voyeur* was politically driven—a system never really tested, yet four years ago, became a springboard—a platform—upon which the President reached the White House. It's already a reelection campaign issue!"

"Bob, would you expect the political opposition to seal their lips when the President faces challenges of this magnitude? I think not!

"There will always be the political pundits, the critics. But let me assure you that the focus of the President is on combating terrorism. No matter what shape, form, or tact. He will do whatever it takes to find those responsible and hold them accountable.

"Yes, there will be a time for politics. That's the system and the privilege we enjoy in this wonderful democracy. But now is neither the time nor the place!

"Marilyn, you have a question?" Cindy offered, as she directed her attention to a *CNN* reporter seated in the third row of the press assembly.

* * * * * *

Noon, Tuesday, April 6, 2004
The Pentagon

Uniformed personnel, *Department of Defense* support staff, and technical specialists occupied every seat in the *Strategic Command Post Planning Room*. In its center, a large semi-circular table faced a podium and wall-sized projection screen.

Along the perimeter of the table, executive style chairs provided seating for each of the chiefs of staff. The desktop in front of each chair was stacked with technical reports and reams of paperwork. Coffee cups, bottled water, and soda cans created the false appearance of a work session in disarray.

For two hours, the chiefs of staff listened as staff specialists and program analysts reviewed system protocols and security checklists. Global reconnaissance, telecommunications, linguistics—no detail, regardless of its significance, was overlooked. Despite their thoroughness, nothing indicated a *Voyeur* malfunction. Still, the reality of world events was staggeringly different.

Standing at the podium, a uniformed technology specialist, speaking with a dry, monotone voice, presented an extraordinarily complex *Voyeur* system report. Holding a laser pointer in his hand, he enumerated a series of three-dimensional graphs on the projection screen. The report seemed never-ending and, at this point, made little sense to anyone, including James Wright.

This guy is killing us, James thought, as he listened to the droning, impersonal recitation. *He's got a voice like Darth Vader with asthma! Where the hell did he come from, anyway? Thank God he's the last one!*

James tilted back in his swivel chair. Fidgeting with a pencil in his hands, he stared over his reading glasses and discretely studied every face in the room. Tired, weary expressions reflected the twelve hours of stress-filled work that had been accomplished since early morning. Still, he knew there was more work to do...much more.

As the officer completed the presentation, James turned to the assembly and for questions. He surveyed the chiefs with his eyes... There were none.

Thank God, he thought.

"Thank you, sir," he said, acknowledging the specialist with a nod of his head. Turning to the chiefs, he addressed the group. "Ladies, gentlemen, I appreciate your patience and the attention you have given the staff. As you know, this is a tedious, but critical process. On top of that, most of you have been up all night.

"We'll take a one hour recess, then reconvene for the *round table* discussion and strategic session. When we reassemble, the *round table* will be restricted to chiefs of staff. Other personnel will be included in the strategic session. Unless there are questions or comments, we are adjourned."

James looked around the room. Hearing no response, he closed the meeting. "We are adjourned."

Responding to the directive, the chiefs and support staff gathered their materials and moved out of the room for the adjournment. Some stood momentarily to discuss work assignments and schedules; others moved quickly out of the room, racing for the restroom, a smoke, or just a breath of fresh air.

Air Force General Robert Pierce occupied the post located two seats to the right of James Wright. As he stood in front of his chair, the air force general gathered a stack of documents from the desktop, placed them in his briefcase, and snapped the brass locks of the luggage. Turning to leave the room, he faced General Wright. "James."

Still seated, James looking up from his work and responded to the general. "Yes, General?"

Recognizing protocol and the countless staff still milling around in the room, the general moved close to General Wright, then surveyed the room quickly to see who might listen to his comments. He spoke in a hushed tone to the chairman.

"James, we've been sitting in these chairs for nearly two hours, listening to staff tell us they don't know what the hell is wrong with *Voyeur*... Yet there was no warning, no intelligence. You don't have to be a *damned rocket scientist* to know the system doesn't work! Last month, Dublin, today, Tel Aviv! *God* knows where it will be tomorrow!"

"You know how I feel about *Voyeur*—political bullsh–"

"We addressed the politics this morning, General!" Wright interrupted.

"No, *you* addressed it this morning! I haven't addressed a damn thing," he said, continuing to speak with a hushed, yet forceful tone.

"Save your remarks for the work session, General!"

"Indeed I will, General ... Indeed I will."

* * * * * *

Air Force Chief Robert Pierce closed the door of his Pentagon office. Turning the brass knob of the deadbolt, he moved from the doorway to his desk and took a seat in the cushioned leather executive style chair. The top of the large mahogany desk was covered with paperwork and folders. The "In Basket" was filled to capacity with documents and folders. Although stacks of paperwork *appeared* to have been neglected for weeks, it was merely the first wave of correspondence he would receive that day.

Leaning forward in his chair, he lifted the telephone receiver from its cradle and from the inside pocket of his uniform jacket, removed a small note pad. Manipulating the leaflet with one hand, he punched in a sequence of numbers from one of its pages. As the telephone made its connection, he leaned back in the chair and listened. An electronic tone signaled the call. Three rings later, a voice answered.

"Yes?"

"Senator?"

"Yes."

"General Pierce. Good afternoon."

"General! And to what do I owe the pleasure of your call?" The sarcasm in the senator's voice was easily detected. Pierce smiled at the inflection in his friend's voice.

"Oh, not much. Just calling to let you know the *chiefs of staff* met a little while ago—same old, same old. Wright doesn't have a clue. The entire *Voyeur* program is a mess—just as we predicted. It's starting to get to him. If you could turn up the pressure a little more, that would be nice!"

"Hey, not a problem. I can handle that."

"I know you can."

"When is the next meeting?"

"Later this afternoon. We'll do a *round table* and then strategic planning. Following that, we work on individual assignments—trouble shooting, system protocols. You know the drill."

"Yeah. Let him spin his wheels! It'll keep him occupied ... Hey, stay in touch. I'll take care of things on this end."

"You got it. I'll talk with you later."

* * * * * *

Oxford, England
Oxford University

Thomas Leed faced the front of the classroom, pointed the handheld remote control at the projection screen, and pressed the power button. Responding to the electronic command, the fan motor of the ceiling-mounted projector whirred softly to life. Spontaneously, an intense white light emerged from the projector lens and, within seconds, its powerful beam illuminated the surface of the wall-mounted screen behind him.

Simultaneously, the professor manipulated the mode selector of the control with the fingers of his right hand. Quickly, he switched the device from auxiliary projection, to video, to audio, then back to projection. Satisfied with the test, he pressed the power button to initiate the "shutdown" sequence.

Good, he thought. *Everything's ready for the class presentations. The students will be elated when these reports are finished. They've all worked hard ... It's been long semester.*

From the technology station, Professor Leed walked to a podium that was positioned midway between the front of the student desks and the projection screen. On the top shelf, under the podium, he placed the remote control, where it would be handy for the students who used *PowerPoint* with their oral report.

With the audiovisual set up out of the way, he opened a black leather brief, which he had placed on top of the podium. From its contents, he retrieved a legal-size yellow pad. Removing a ballpoint pen from his coat pocket, he used the writing instrument as a guide as he studied the notes written on the top page.

"Today, we have four reports—Robert, Elizabeth, James and Thomas," he recounted to himself. "These are the last of the student presentations."

"We'll start with a class discussion of current events, then take a short break before we begin the reports. Following the reports, we'll finish with a review for the final exam ... That will do it for today."

Satisfied with the lesson plan, Professor Leed placed the pad inside the brief. Noting the time on the wall clock, he made a calculation. *Eight forty-five; fifteen minutes before we begin—enough time for a coffee refill and the lavatory,* he thought.

Coffee mug in hand, he turned to walk toward the classroom door. As he reached for the brass knob, the door swung open. There, standing in the doorway was one of his students, Jaime Patterson.

Jaime was never tardy, and, like today, usually the first student to arrive at class. Dressed in black corduroy jeans, she wore a black cotton sweater and white blouse.

Black-leather ankle-high boots completed the attire. Over her shoulder, she carried a book pack. The handle of a small umbrella protruded from one of its labyrinthine compartments.

Jaime was a bright, attractive girl in her mid-twenties. Long, dark brown hair and eyes complimented her tall, slender frame. Although she was popular with the guys, Jaime was a serious student who made her studies a priority. Opening the door, she greeted the professor with a smile.

"Good morning, Professor Leed."

"Good morning, Jaime. How are you today?"

"Quite good," she replied. "I'll be glad to see the end of the semester, though. I'm taking eighteen hours, and it's a wee bit of a load."

"Eighteen!" he exclaimed. "That is quite much, don't you think, particularly in *your* degree program?"

"Aye, sir. But if I can do that again in the fall semester, I'll finish my program. I'm anxious to start a career. I've been a full time student since my undergraduate days. You know what I mean?"

"Oh, yes, my dear. I know what you mean. And you have so much to look forward to...so many opportunities. You will do well; whatever you choose."

Raising his coffee mug toward her, he exclaimed. "If you'll excuse me, I'll be right back. I'm on my way to refill my coffee...before we begin."

"Aye, sir ... See you in a short."

Again, Thomas turned to leave the classroom when another student, Robert Tanner, entered the room.

"Good morning, Professor."

"Good morning, Robert. Ready with your report?"

"Oh, yes, sir! I'm using PowerPoint, but I'm not sure about the auxiliary projection. Could you assist me with the connection?"

"Certainly. Let's see what you've got."

Professor Leed walked back to the podium, still holding the empty coffee mug in hand. The refill and lavatory would have to wait. With just minutes before the start of class, there was not enough time for the break and still assist the student with the computer projection set-up.

As the professor worked with Robert, other students entered the room. By class time, all were in their seats, engaged in small talk as they waited for the professor to call the class to order.

With the projector connections in place, Robert thanked the professor and moved to a vacant seat near the back of the classroom.

"Good morning, students," Professor Leed announced, extending a greeting to the class. "I see there is a lot of energy this morning. Could it be we are anxious to see the semester come to an end? One more class, you know...then the final."

The students smiled at the professor and chuckled.

"No!" one of the students retorted. "Give us more! We're into human misery and suffering!"

The class erupted in laughter.

"Ah, I'm sure you are, and *I'm* the *'task master'*!" the professor proclaimed, continuing the good-natured exchange. "But enough for now, time for work! There's a lot that we must do. We'll begin with a discussion of current events, then following a break, the last of the reports—Robert, first, then Elizabeth, James and Thomas... We'll finish with a review for the final, and that should do it!"

Thomas placed the note pad back inside the brief and from a file folder, removed the class attendance sign-in sheet. Without speaking, he handed the form to a female student seated in a front row desk. At this point in the semester, there was no need for verbal directions; recording class attendance was a matter of routine.

Surveying the students with his eyes, Thomas began the discussion.

"Who would like to begin? Who has a current event topic to discuss," he queried.

"Tel Aviv!"

The shouted response came from Jonathan McCleary, slouched in his seat at the back of the room. Jonathan wore jeans and a sweatshirt that displayed the logo of an expensive, yet popular, clothes designer.

On the floor, next to his desk, was a book bag and umbrella. Jonathan was a second-year graduate student majoring in political science. The son of a wealthy businessman, he was ostensibly affluent.

Early in the semester, Jonathan established his snobby, "know-it-all" reputation when he announced to the class his career plan to become a wealthy attorney—*not that he needed the money!*

At any given time, a short conversation with Jonathan revealed an opinionated, sarcastic, and conceited personality. By this point in the semester, most of the class had had enough of Jonathan.

Simultaneously, the class rolled their eyes and shared quick glances to one another in response to his retort.

"Tel Aviv!" Professor Leed responded. "Tell us about Tel Aviv, Jonathan."

"Why don't *you* tell *us*, professor?" he replied sarcastically, skillfully walking the line of disrespect. "Aren't you an authority on *Voyeur*? Wasn't that system designed to intercept terrorist communication *prior to* a launched attack?"

Understanding the personality of the student, Professor Leed always took the "high road" in matters of confrontation. Ignoring the indignation, he replied. "Authority? Well, about that, I can't say. As all of you know," turning his gaze to the students, "I *was* involved in the development of *Voyeur*. And yes, the system is programmed to intercept aggressive intelligence associated with terrorism. But these systems, all of them, are vulnerable to imperfection."

"Well, from what I understand," Jonathan retorted. "President Stone presented *Voyeur* to the international community as a perfect system. The ultimate global defense against terrorism... It all sounds political to me! Obviously, the system has failed!"

Spontaneously, from across the room, Elizabeth Stall countered the indictment. "Failed? And how do *you* know the system has failed?"

"When something doesn't work, it has failed...broken... The system has failed," he replied with indignation.

"Still, how do you know it's the *system*? There are a multitude of explanations for what might have happened."

"Like what?"

"Conspiracy, for one! The system may have been manipulated!"

"Yeah right, girl. You're just defending the professor... and *Voyeur*. It's political; all of it...has been from the start. The system doesn't work. The system failed!"

"Students! I appreciate your ideas...and no one is, or needs, to defend me! What happened in Tel Aviv, we don't know. Obviously, it is a disturbing and critically important situation; one that we will monitor. In the end, I imagine we will know if the system works. In the meantime, we'll take a short break before we begin the reports."

Turning his attention to a student seated near the front of the class, Professor Leed directed. "Robert, you will give the first report."

"Yes, sir."

"Let's take a short break."

* * * * * *

The private line to the senator's office rang once before he picked up the receiver. The senator answered, "Yes," then listened carefully to the voice at the other end of the line.

"I thought we agreed you would not call me at my office, much less use this number!" the senator retorted with irritation. "It's too much of a risk!"

"Relax," the voice replied calmly. "Everything is fine. Everything is fine."

"Maybe, but I don't want you calling this number. Besides, what's up?"

"We need to make a money transfer soon."

"Already? When?"

"Not for a couple of weeks, but you need to line things up. Everything must be in place by the end of the month. That's the agreement we have."

"How much this time?"

"Seven-fifty."

"Seven hundred-fifty thousand! Jesus Christ! That's more than we paid for Tel Aviv! What's going on?"

"Look, I know... I know. *Al Qaida* gets the job done, but they don't come cheap, particularly if we score on the Mexican president. Besides, you're the one who wants to be in the White House."

"How much more is this whole thing going to cost? We *never* talked this kind of money! I've got to be careful!"

"This will do it. With the money you've raised, your campaign account can handle it. It will never be missed. The people handling the transfer will make it appear to have come out of nowhere."

"Still, we need to be careful. No more phone calls! I'll get the money. We'll handle it like before."

"Just like before," the voice replied. "Just like before. Oh, by the way, *Happy Holidays*, Senator...I mean, Mr. President!"

* * * * * *

Oxford, England
Oxford University

"Give it all you've got, girl! Snap your foot at the target when you kick ... You can do it! You can *do* it," he urged!

Elizabeth Stall listened intently to her instructor's words. Then, with a nod of her head, acknowledged his order. Concentrating every ounce of mental energy she could muster, she focused on the hand-sized training pad in front of his chest. Quickly, she glanced at the floor and calculated the distance across the padded training mat to the target. Like an Olympic high jumper preparing mentally to clear the bar, she visualized the sequence of steps and the jump-kick she would make.

"You go, girl!" her instructor shouted.

With the command, an extraordinary state of mind enveloped her. Everything around her seemed to move in slow motion. The target that loomed before her appeared bigger and closer than ever.

Over the last year and a half, Elizabeth had maintained a rigid kick-box training schedule at the Oxford University Fitness Center—three practice sessions per week, coupled daily with weight training and a two-mile run.

As one of the newer facilities on campus, the center offered Oxford students and faculty the opportunity to train, exercise, and maintain their physical fitness while in school. Aerobic classes, martial arts, kick-box, and weight training attracted university men and women of all ages. After months of training, the disciplined routine had honed her body into top shape. But the regimen became addictive, and now her sense of fitness so keen that her body couldn't do without it.

Instinctively, Elizabeth moved into position and from a crouched position, hop-stepped swiftly across the mat toward her instructor. The exercise was not easy, but the training and regimented workouts had prepared her mentally and physically for the strenuous maneuver. At a predetermined point, she coiled her petite, 115-pound body and leapt explosively from the floor. The energy from the powerful jump lifted her vertically, more than three feet above the mat. Simultaneously, Elizabeth tilted her head and shoulders back, then downward. Responding to the gymnastic-like technique, her body assumed a "laid out" prone position, parallel to the floor.

Elizabeth wore a white, martial arts robe, tied at the waist with a black sash. Its loose, comfortable fit enabled her to move with total freedom. At the pinnacle of the leap, she cocked her legs with both knees touching her chest. Then with precise timing, she unleashed her feet and kicked violently at the target. Slightly above the mark, the right foot glanced off the training pad and with a loud "smack," hit the face of her instructor squarely between the eyes.

Caught by surprise, the blow came too quickly for him to respond. Like a slow motion replay, his facial expression contorted. Simultaneously, both eyes glazed over as they rolled back in his head. Expelling a soft gasp of air from his lungs, the instructor's legs folded as he collapsed and fell backward onto the mat.

Elizabeth had knocked him out!

Still in the air, Elizabeth prepared for the fall to the floor. Grasping her arms, she hugged her chest, dropped her left shoulder and gritted her teeth. A second later, she hit the mat with a jolt.

With the impact, a flood of emotion enveloped her. But the feeling of exhilaration was overwhelmed by concern for her instructor. Picking herself up from the mat, she raced quickly to him, kneeling by his side. Frantically, she struggled to remove her boxing gloves, then reached to hold his hand.

"Richard! Richard! Are you okay?"

When he didn't respond, Elizabeth became emotional.

"Somebody! Somebody...please help!" she cried.

But help was already there. The impact of her kick and the

subsequent collapse of her instructor attracted the attention of a nearby group of students and their coach. Without hesitation, the coach ran to his colleague and knelt down to diagnose his condition. Within moments, a crowd gathered from throughout the gym. Standing silently, the group encircled Elizabeth and her trainer as the coach administered first aid.

After what seemed an eternity to Elizabeth, her instructor's head began to move; slowly at first, then he opened his eyes.

"Whoa," he mumbled, squinting his eyes to focus. He mumbled again, "Whoa, what happened? What hit me?"

"Elizabeth hit you, old chap...your *student*! You taught her well, my friend," replied the coach.

"Is he all right?" Elizabeth exclaimed. "Will he be okay?"

"Ah, he's fine! Just got his 'bell rung' is all. He's okay. By the way, nice kick!"

Having regained consciousness, Richard replied to his friend's remark. "That's easy for you to say, mate. Let her kick *you* and then tell me how *you* feel!"

With the words of her coach, Elizabeth again became emotional. "Richard, I'm so sorry!" she cried. "I didn't mean to kick *you*! I meant to hit the target. My foot must have... glanced off..."

"Hey... I'm fine, girl. This is not the first time I've had my bell rung," he said, moving to a sitting position on the floor. "And I'm sure, it won't be the last, not with students like you! Good show, Elizabeth! Good show! What say we take a break, huh? You dress in and do your run... I think I'll call it a day."

"You sure you're okay?"

"I'm fine."

Leaning over, Elizabeth kissed him softly on the forehead and whispered. "I'm sorry."

"Not a problem," he replied. "You go... Do your run. I'll be fine."

"Yes, sir. I'll do my run."

Elizabeth stood as two male students assisted the coach in helping Richard to a standing position. Looking back over her shoulder at Richard, she turned and walked to the women's locker room.

Inside the room, Elizabeth paused to take a couple deep breaths. Although Richard appeared to be okay, she was still shaken by the incident. Collecting her wits, she took a seat on the bench in front of her locker and exchanged her kick-box attire for running shoes, shorts and sweatshirt.

"Hey! Nice kick on your coach. You put his lights out, girl! I'll have to give you more respect from now on!"

Turning to the sound of the voice, Elizabeth recognized a good friend and classmate, Krista Jones.

"Hey, girl!" Elizabeth replied. "I have no idea where that came from ... It just happened!"

"Yeah, right. I've been watching you practice. You're getting pretty good. *Very* good in fact!"

"Thanks. I appreciate the compliment. I just hope Richard is okay."

"Richard? Are you kidding me? His head is as hard as a gourd. You ought to see the licks he takes from the guys. He'll be fine. If anything, you better worry about your foot," she laughed.

"Yeah, right. Hey, you want to run with me?"

"Thanks, but I can't this time. I've got a study group to catch in a few minutes...over at the library. Maybe another time ... I'd love to."

"Hey, not a problem. We'll do it next time."

"Great!"

Elizabeth tied the laces of her shoes, closed the gym locker door, and headed for the street exit. Moments later, her feet were pounding the sidewalk pavement, marking time for the thirty-minute run.

Elizabeth's route took her from the *Westgate Shopping Centre*, east along Queen Street. At a brisk pace, she crossed Cornmarket, following a route with which she was keenly familiar. With each stride, she could anticipate every crack in the sidewalk, pothole, or incline. Having run the route so many times, her body had developed a keen sensitivity to changes in the slope of the road. No matter how slight, her body told her when she was running "uphill" or "down." The longer the run, the more sensitive it was to the subtle changes. Soon, her body found its rhythm and the minutes ticked away. As she ran, Elizabeth listened to a favorite CD through her Sony headset. The relaxing music enabled her to establish a consistent stride.

Enjoying the pace, she marveled at the classic buildings, church spires, and gothic architecture that framed her route. Inspired by their timeless beauty, she quickly found herself enveloped in the spirit of Oxford. John Wyclif, Edmund Halley, John and Charles Wesley, John Locke, Thomas Huxley, Lewis Carroll were icons among the annals of Oxford history; men whose writings, philosophies, and discoveries stand as legacies among mankind. She could imagine the great debates...the discourse...the discoveries! Knowing that she was a part of that rich heritage filled her with pride.

Turning left on Catte, her route took her north to Broad Street. At Broad Street, she turned west, past *Flaggs - the College Store*, across Magdelaun to George Street. George Street was the halfway point, from there, she would turn south and retrace her route to the gym.

What a day, she thought. *Tel Aviv, Professor Leed's class, teaching the undergraduate class and now, knocking out my instructor!* "I don't need this," she exclaimed. "Perhaps, I'll stop by the *Lamb and Flag* for a draught after my run.

"I can't believe the way Jonathan McCleary addressed Professor Leed this morning about *Voyeur*. His sarcasm makes me want to throw up. That rich little bastard. He makes me sick! Smart-ass! Spending... no, *wasting* his daddy's money on college. Thinks he knows it all...has all the answers! Professor Leed handled it well...he always does; he's great!"

Elizabeth's thoughts of Professor Leed were fresh in her mind as she looked ahead along George Street. There, in the distance, she recognized a familiar figure at the front of the Department of Politics and International Relations Building.

"Professor Leed!" she exclaimed to herself.

Dressed in a black topcoat, the Professor wore a dark tweed hat with a wool scarf wrapped around his neck.

"I'll bet he's on his way home for the day."

Elizabeth slowed her pace as she approached her mentor and

friend.

"Professor Leed!" she shouted.

Turning his head to face her, the professor smiled and returned the greeting. "Elizabeth! Young lady, I'm happy to see you are staying in shape enough to keep up with me," he joked with a smile. "Finishing your workout for the day, I presume?"

"Yes, sir. Part of the routine, you know. Can't let you get ahead of me," she teased. "Professor Leed, I'm sorry about class this morning."

"Sorry? And what is there for *you* to be sorry about?"

"You know. If you don't mind my saying, sir, he's a spoiled rich kid! A brat who thinks he knows it all. Just put him in a situation like they are at the Pentagon and see how *he* handles it! I'll bet he'd be the first one to... Well, I can't say all that I would like to say... His sarcastic attitude makes me sick!"

"Hey, don't worry about it. If nothing else, it makes the class interesting. There's always something to learn from opposing views. Sometimes I'm not sure what that might *be*, but something...probably."

"Well, Professor, I just wanted you to know how I felt about it... And the way you handled it ...and everything."

"Thank you, Elizabeth, but don't worry about it."

"I'll finish the research reports this evening and have them ready for you tomorrow. It's been a lot of work, but I've learned a lot!"

"Good! You've worked hard and I look forward to reading the research. I'll see you in the morning."

"Yes, sir, in the morning. See ya!"

"Take care."

* * * * * *

Thursday, April 15, 2004
Orange County, California

From her position by the classroom door, first-year Orange County High School Spanish teacher Maria Gonzales glances at the clock on the wall. It is 7:00 p.m.

As she walks to the chalkboard at the front of the room, she studies the audience. A parent or student occupies each of the twenty-five desks. At the back of the room, seated in a student desk, is her school assistant principal, Michael Kelly. Travel posters of Mexico, Spain and Latin America scenes decorate the room. From the ceiling in the back of the room hangs a piñata. The décor creates points of interest for students trying to understand a second language.

Again, she notes the faces and, though many are unfamiliar, she recognizes their smiles of anticipation. Each expression reflects excitement for the upcoming class trip to Mexico City and the *Cinco de Mayo* celebration.

Standing before the group, she displays confidence and poise. Her physical appearance is stunning; black hair and dark brown eyes compliment a smooth complexion and natural beauty.

Although she is a rookie teacher, her Latin heritage has enhanced her professional training and instructional assignment. It is her charisma, though, that attracts students and parents alike.

Maria is inexperienced in speaking to adult audiences. That makes her nervous, but still, she is anxious to begin. With her hand, she directs their attention to the words on the chalkboard. Smiling, she points to the phrase and speaks with a clear, crisp enunciation. *"Buenos dias!"*

Eliciting a response, she nods her head to the assembly. Spontaneously, they respond, "Buenos dias!"

Again, she leads: "Como esta?"

"Como esta?" they echo.

"Muy bien, gracias!"

"Muy bien, gracias!"

Smiling and with a chuckle, she praises them in English: "Very good! Very, *very* good!"

"Good evening, parents and students! My name is Maria Gonzales. On behalf of the Orange County High School Spanish Club and our assistant principal, Senior...*Mr*....Michael Kelly, it is my privilege to welcome you to our parent orientation meeting for the class field trip to Mexico."

She points to her colleague at the back of the room, who smiles and nods his head in acknowledgment.

"I can see in your faces that everyone is excited about the trip. I am excited, too, and look forward to sharing this experience with you. If you look at the itinerary on the blue sheet of paper at your desk, we can review the travel schedule together."

The group responds, self-directing its attention to the printed document.

"As you know, a highlight of the trip is our visit to Mexico City and the Cinco de Mayo celebration. My family and associates living in Mexico City have made arrangements for the class to participate in the celebration parade."

The audience applauds.

"Celebrities and dignitaries from the government, including the President of Mexico and members of his staff, will be there. We may have the opportunity to be introduced to the President. For many of us it will be the trip of a lifetime."

This time the audience applauds vigorously as several groups of parents and students engage in small talk. To recapture their attention, she pauses briefly before continuing. A student, seated at the front of the room, raises her hand. Displaying an obvious enthusiasm for the trip, she does not wait to be acknowledged by the teacher.

"Miss Gonzales, will it be okay if I bring a radio or CD player on the tour bus?"

With the remark, the beaming audience chuckles, focusing their attention on the student, then back to the teacher.

"Yes, of course, Amy," Miss Gonzales responds with a smile. "As long as it doesn't create a distraction or problem for others. In fact, I'm glad that you asked that question. I was going to discuss the list of *Items to Bring* on the second page of the handout. We can do that now."

The orientation progresses as the teacher reviews the itinerary, travel schedule, food and hotel accommodations. Numerous questions are asked, and in each case she responds with patience and understanding.

As questions are exhausted, the meeting draws to a close. Then a mother seated at the front of the room next to her young daughter raises her hand.

Moving closer to read the letters printed on the *Hello My Name Is* badge attached to the blouse of the parent, Ms. Gonzales notes her name and smiles in response. "Yes, Mrs....Mrs. Johnson."

"Yes, Ms. Gonzales, thank you. The parents, and especially the kids, are excited about the trip. We have observed your first year as a new teacher to our school. I know I speak for the group in saying how grateful we are for the work you do for our children."

Spontaneously, the room explodes with intense applause. Obviously embarrassed by the attention, Ms. Gonzales nods in appreciation.

"Thank you ... Thank you."

Placing her left hand on her daughter's shoulder, the parent continues. "But...well...for many of us...for many of the students...this is their first trip away from home, especially a trip out of the country."

The mother looks affectionately at her daughter, then back to Ms. Gonzales. "Will the students be closely supervised? I mean...well...for their safety?"

For the first time, without prompt, the group is silent. Though unspoken, it is clear that world events and the safety of their children are ever-present in the minds of the parents.

Pausing, she pans the faces as she considers her response. Showing no anxiety, she looks into their eyes and speaks with compassion. "Mrs. Johnson, that is an important question. In fact, it is a question that I am glad you asked before we dismissed.

"As teachers and parents, we share a common concern for our students...our children. Too often, the world in which we live is not what we want it to be.

"A field trip, any trip, especially one that is out of the country, is an important responsibility for teachers and chaperones. Our visit to Mexico is one for which you have entrusted me with the care of your children.

"As you know, many parents and students in this room have worked hard and devoted countess hours to ensure this is a positive experience for everyone. While none of us can guarantee absolute safety, I have confidence that, collectively, we have been conscientious in this area of responsibility.

"There will be one adult chaperone for every three students and, as a group, we will be together throughout the trip. I believe the children will be as safe as we can make them and will have many fond memories to share with their friends when we return..."

* * * * * *

Mexico City—The Presidential Palace
The Presidential Garden

President Carlos Sanchez walked slowly as he followed the cobblestone pathway that meandered through the *Presidential Garden*. Pushed by a slight breeze, the cool morning air felt fresh to his face. He was relaxed and comfortable, dressed in a light, natural-colored linen suit, cotton shirt, silk tie, and soft lizard skinned loafers.

The President was a tall man with dark eyes and aquiline nose. Black, collar-length hair and mustache, both neatly trimmed, gave his sixty-year-old frame a handsome, yet distinctive appearance.

Lining both sides of the narrow trail, an aurora of flowering plants and exotic cacti created a corridor of breathtaking color. Cast by the walls of the Presidential Palace, the waning shadows offered a temporary haven for the early morning dew that adorned the foliage. Soon, the rising Mexican sun and its ruthless heat would evaporate the precious moisture, claiming its vapor as its first victim of the day.

For Carlos, the morning ritual was a time of solitude. It was his favorite time of the day. But despite its fleeting moments, there was no haste to his movement and he paused often to examine the flowers and colorful blooms. Ignoring their familiarity, he scrutinized each one carefully as though it were new discovery.

Behind him, at a discreet distance, a member of the Presidential security unit monitored his routine. For the President of Mexico, private moments were uncommon; rarities to be savored, like the swallow of a fine wine. But that was okay; at least for now. One day, he would reclaim his personal life. Now, there was work to do and he felt a sense of purpose as the leader of his nation.

The economy was doing well and a free trade agreement with the United States held great promise for new jobs and increased productivity. Indeed, his popularity with the people was at its highest point ever.

But success in politics doesn't come without a price; at least not in Mexico. Political trade offs and "gentlemen's agreements" were the way you conducted business if you were to advance your political agenda.

Still, the dark cloud of drug trafficking and the ever-present threat of terrorism overshadowed the good times. Much had been accomplished since the tragedy in New York, but recent events in Dublin and Tel Aviv reminded him of the relentless nature of evil. When would it end?

As the President completed his routine, he made his way along the path to the stairway that led to the private entrance of the Palace and the Presidential office. Holding the stair rail for balance, he stepped carefully to the top level. There, standing by the door, was his staff assistant, Juanita Fuentes.

"Buenos dias, Senior Presidente."

"Buenos dias, Juanita."

"Senior Presidente, I'm sorry to disturb you, but General Gozales has asked to see you."

"But, Juanita, you are not disturbing me! I just finished my morning walk. The garden is beautiful, as always!"

"Si, senior. It is always beautiful. It's your pride and joy, Senior Presidente!"

"Please have the General come to my office. We'll have coffee!"

"Si, senior."

The President made his way down the hallway and stood by his office door, waiting to greet the deputy chief of staff and good friend, Guierrmo Gonzales. Moments later, the tall frame of the uniformed general appeared.

"Buenos dias, Guierrmo. Como esta?"

"Muy bien, gracias. Senior Presidente. Y usted?"

"Ah, muy bien. Muy bien. Café?"

Together, they walked to a table near the back office wall and window that overlooked the garden and palace grounds. Pausing briefly, they stood shoulder-to-shoulder gazing at the palace grounds and distant terrain. Across the landscape, a thin shroud of fog, clinging desperately to pockets of low-lying vegetation, hugged the ground. Soon, in a hopeless struggle against the rays of the sun, the last vestiges of morning would be taken.

Moving to the coffee table, the Presidente poured two steaming cups of dark Colombian blend. Passing one cup to the general, the Presidente gestured to an ornate silver pitcher of cream and bowl of sugar. Ignoring the condiments, both men raised their cups in a morning toast before taking their first swallow.

"Umm…muy bien," the Presidente remarked. "And how may I help you, mi amigo?"

"Si! Muchas gracias. Senior Presidente, I have a favor to ask, por favor."

"Si, but of course. Anything for you, mi amigo."

"Next month at the Cinco de Mayo celebration—the parade—would you consider having a group of Americano students and my niece, Maria, their teacher, accompany your party in the parade?

"There are a dozen students, my niece and two other chaperones," the general continued. "They are visiting Mexico City as a class trip. She called me last night to ask if you would consider allowing them to walk in the parade."

"Oh, but of course, Guiermmo. It will be my pleasure. But they need not walk! We will provide an automobile and feature them as our guests. It will be a great opportunity to promote our friendship with the citizens of the United States."

"Mr. Presidente, I am grateful for your gesture. This is much more than Maria could have ever expected. I don't want to impose, but she will be honored when I share this news with her!"

"Why of course! It will be my pleasure. I look forward to meeting her and the students. It will be wonderful!"

* * * * * *

Downtown - Mexico City
An Inner-City Neighborhood

Exposure to the harsh, subtropical Mexico City environment had taken its toll on the inner-city apartment complex. Cracked paint on the exterior stucco walls was faded and peeling, having suffered through years of neglect. Withering tropical plants and flowers that once proudly adorned the building grounds, now lay weed-choked and withered. In their place was a ghetto-like landscape of trash, newspapers, and broken bottles, where unleashed dogs and stray cats competed for discarded scraps and garbage.

In the kitchen of one of the second floor units, four men, dressed in military-like garb, huddled around a table. From the ceiling, a single lamp fixture, suspended by a frail electrical cord, cast its dim light. A detailed map of Mexico City was spread across the table. Focusing their attention on a schematic diagram, the listened intently to the words of their leader Raheem Rashad.

Raheem stood at one end of the table with the black, military laced boot of his left foot positioned in the seat of a chair. Leaning over the map, he placed his left forearm across his leg for balance. Although he spoke fluent Spanish, his short dark hair, black eyes, and Mid-Eastern features distinguished him from his Hispanic companions. With a fixed-blade military style knife, he pointed to the features on the map. The group of anxious, yet willing conspirators listened intently as he explained the plan.

"Pedro, you will drive the panel truck to this location," he said, pointing with the tip of the knife to a parking space on *Paseo de la Reforma*, directly across from the *Palacio de Nacional*. "This is within a half block of the parade review stand. The outside of the truck will be painted white with the *City of Mexico* logo and *Public Works Department* prominently displayed on both sides.

"There will be many service vehicles in the area like this one. As long as you act like you are preparing for the parade, no one will pay attention to you or the vehicle, including the policia! The truck will be loaded with the explosives.

"Miguel," he continued, gesturing with the knife to the young, dark-haired man with a mustache seated to his right. "You will ride with Pedro. Both of you will wear the blue, *Public Works Department* jumpsuits over your street clothes. Once the truck is positioned, activate the cell phone, place it on the floorboard in front of the microphone, and lock the truck.

"Remember, remove the orange parking cones from the cab and place them in front of and behind the vehicle. This setup will give the appearance that you are preparing for the parade cleanup. Remember, again, there will be many vehicles like the one you will be driving, so don't feel as though everyone will be watching you.

"When you have positioned the parking cones, walk casually along the sidewalk. By this time, there will be many people who have gathered to watch the parade. It will be easy for you to blend into the crowd. From the *Palacio*, you will go south four blocks and then east for two.

"Juan, you will drive the green pickup truck to this location." He pointed to a street intersection on the map. "Park here," he indicated with the knife, "at the end of the second block."

Looking directly at Juan, Raheem continued, "You will have a cell phone and the clothes bag. Wait for Pedro and Miguel. By the time they arrive, there will be less than 30 minutes before the parade begins. Tune the truck radio to the 900 AM station. It will broadcast the parade review. Your cue is the point at which the announcer recognizes President Sanchez and his entourage."

Again, Raheem pointed to a specific location on the map with his knife. "This places them at 'ground zero' for the explosion. Pedro, Miguel. Remember, you *must* remove the jumpsuits and place them in the clothes bag as soon as you are inside the pickup. This is important to ensure there is no attention directed to you when you leave the truck!

"The pickup will be parked at a safe distance, but when the explosives are detonated, you will experience a shock wave from the blast. DON'T LET THIS DISTRACT YOU FROM THE PLAN! Every procedure must be followed as I have directed! Is this clear?"

The three men nodded their heads indicating they understood.

"Once the detonation has occurred, Pedro will drive carefully, without speeding, back to this apartment. You will park the truck across the street. Place the clothes bag in the green trash disposal in the alley, and meet me here.

"I will monitor the parade with my radio. Once I hear the explosion, I will be waiting and ready for you. Our rendezvous point with another vehicle and driver is three blocks from here.

"Quickly, we will gather our things and be gone. Are there questions?"

Simultaneously, the three men shook their heads, indicating they understood. Acknowledging their response, Raheem offered refreshments. "Good! There is Dos XX in the refrigerator and I have Tequila. Let's drink!"

Within an hour, the four terrorists transformed the kitchen table into a shrine of empty Dos XX beer bottles. Its centerpiece was a near-empty quart bottle of Jose' Quervo, four shot glasses, and an opened bag of oft-neglected tortilla chips. Having consumed a substantial quantity of alcohol, Miguel, who sat at the opposite end of the table from Raheem, leaned forward with his elbows on the table, the chin of his head propped in his hands. Rhythmically, his eyes blinked slowly in a sleepy droop as he listened to the animated conversation of Pedro and Juan.

Through moderation, Raheem maintained a clear head; not that he didn't enjoy the liquor, but there was work to do before the evening was over. Pushing back from the table, he rose from his chair to leave the room.

"Compadres, enjoy this time together…and the liquor. We will not have opportunities like this any time soon."

Turning to leave the kitchen, he addressed the men. "Please excuse me as I have work to do in the other room."

Simultaneously, the three conspirators raised their hands to the leader in a "high five" gesture of gratitude. Smiling, Raheem moved to each of the men and grasped the palm of their hand in return.

"Gracias, me amigos... Gracias!"

From the kitchen, Raheem walked to the living room where a ragged, cloth-covered couch and two chairs were positioned on opposite sides of the room. In one corner, a television occupied the surface of a small table. Across the room, next to the window, was an oak desk and chair. On top of the desk were a carry-on size piece of luggage and a small leather briefcase.

Raheem moved across the room to the desk, popped the latches of the luggage and removed a radio transmitter, a compact satellite dish antenna, and several pieces of electronic equipment. Within moments, he assembled the communication device, opened the window, and positioned the satellite on the sill.

Sitting at the desk, he placed a headset with microphone over his ears, connected them to the transmitter, and flipped the toggle power switch to the *On* position. As the unit powered up, Raheem retrieved a small spiral bound notepad from the luggage. Flipping through the leaflet, he scrutinized a series of the figures scrawled on one of the pages. Studying the numbers, he punched in the frequency settings of the tuner. Satisfied with the configuration, he moved his hand to the transmitter lever. When he heard the *send* prompt in the headset, he dispatched the message.

"*Cinco de Mayo* is a go. Money transfer requested. Happy Holidays!"

Having completed the task, Raheem dismantled the equipment and placed the items back in the luggage. Standing in front of the desk, he positioned the chair under the desk. Bending slightly at the waist, he grasped the bottom right hand drawer of the desk and pulled it from its tray.

From the leather brief, Raheem removed a leather pouch and

placed it carefully in a hollow compartment behind the desk drawer. Replacing the drawer, he secured the locks on the luggage and walked back to the kitchen to join his companions.

* * * * * *

Chesapeake Bay, Maryland
Tilgham Island

With the passion of a Latin lover, the red Porsche hugged the serpentine curves of the two-lane highway. At each switchback, the driver downshifted the manual transmission, prompting the engine to whine like a spoiled child.

For countless miles, the coastline manipulated the meandering roadway, all the while maintaining its relentless grip on the tempestuous sports car. Then, as though conceding, the road unfolded into a straightaway, offering its captive a token moment of freedom. Seizing the opportunity, the driver pushed the throttle dangerously close to its redline. Within moments the sleek automobile consumed the mile-long stretch of blacktop.

Placing her hand on his, Susan Wright squeezed her husband's arm. "Okay '*Mario*,' I know you have enough stress for the both of us, but I'd like to enjoy our Maryland crab dinner in one piece."

Glancing at his wife, James Wright smiled. "Sorry about that," he replied, backing off the accelerator. "You *know* I love this car ... sometimes I just get caught up in myself."

For the past hour, James and Susan had traveled south on U.S. Highway 50, then west from Easton, Maryland, on State Road 33. The couple followed the scenic route along the eastern shore of Chesapeake Bay, where it transverses a prominent, but crooked, finger-like peninsula. Near its end, the road crosses a short span of drawbridge at Knapps Narrows to Tilgham Island and the quaint villages of Tilgham and Fairbanks.

Tilgham Island is located in the mid-Chesapeake Bay region.

Travelers to the area describe its two communities, Tilgham and Fairbanks, as true working watermen's villages, where excellent fishing abounds. Just minutes from historic St. Michaels, Oxford and Easton, the village of Tilgham is renowned as the home of the last sailing fleet in North America, the *Skipjacks*.

With its proximity to cities like Washington D.C., Baltimore, Philadelphia, and Annapolis, the island attracts countless visitors seeking respite from the rigors of urban life. During his assignment in Washington, D.C., James and Susan were frequent visitors to Tilgham Island. It was their *"get-a-way"*; a place where anniversaries, Mother's Day, or birthday weekends could be enjoyed in anonymity.

For several minutes, the couple did not speak, taking time to enjoy the fresh air, sunshine, and mesmerizing whine of the powerful sports car. As they drew closer to their destination, James resumed the conversation.

"God, it's a beautiful day! Can you believe we're getting away for the weekend...especially with everything that's going on? And tonight, that crab dinner...among other things." He smiled. "It's going to be great! I can't wait to get to the *Skipjack Inn* and eat at the *Narrows!*"

Returning his smile, Susan replied, "I know work has been tough. You'll figure it out, James. I *know* you will! Let's just enjoy the weekend and time together."

For several miles, James drove silently along the coastal highway, lost in his thoughts and enjoying the landscape. Then, turning to Susan, he continued the conversation. "It's been a while since we ate at the *Narrows*...and the *Inn* is always neat. Bob and Judy are terrific."

"They're a wonderful couple and great friends. And, James, I've *got* to check out the shops. You never can tell where I might find a bargain."

"By all means! If anyone can find a bargain, you'll be the one." He smiled.

With his right hand, James squeezed the palm of Susan's hand. "I love you, Susan."

"I love you, too, James," she said, smiling as she returned the squeeze.

"Hey, I see the bridge! Almost there," James shouted as he slowed the Porsche for the crossing over the drawbridge at Knapps Narrows.

As they passed the Knapps Narrows Marina on the island side of the narrow waterway, James noted a fleet of fishing boats and cruisers parked along the dock. Each vessel proudly sported the name of someone—or something—on its bow that held special meaning to its owner.

For several years, as a hobby, James "collected" the names of boats. He couldn't recall how he got into the notion of writing down the names, but the idea intrigued him. Before long, it became a hobby of sorts. Although he never counted, he imagined his collection totaled more than a thousand different names.

In some strange way, collecting boat names was a scavenger hunt, like Trivial Pursuit, something to occupy his mind. This weekend, he was certain to add several new entries to his collection. Perhaps, one day, he might write a book about the names and some of the extraordinary stories behind them.

As James directed his thoughts to the things around him, he felt tension leave his body. Finally, he was beginning to relax. Spending quality time with Susan was the therapy he desperately needed.

Gazing up the road, James recognized the Skipjack Inn. The bed and breakfast would be their retreat for the weekend. Each of its twenty bedrooms was unique, and Susan looked forward to trying a different room each time.

James turned the Porsche into the parking lot; pulling up to a space marked "Registration Parking." Switching off the engine, he reached in the backseat for a briefcase that contained his wallet, cell phone, notepad, road map, and personal telephone directory.

"I'll check us in, then come back for the luggage."

"Thanks," Susan replied. "I'll get my things together. I need to freshen my make-up. Tell Bob and Judy I'll see them in a few minutes."

"You look great," James smiled. "You don't have to worry about the make-up... I'll be right back."

Since their first visit to Tilgham Island, James and Susan had established a friendship with Innkeepers Bob and Judy Fairbanks. Nearly ten years ago, having completed successful careers in the financial industry, Bob and Judy "retired" to Tilgham Island. Their plan was to invest a portion of their good fortune in a bed and breakfast establishment.

At the same time, a realtor in Easton posted a listing for the Skipjack Inn. Ironically, it was their favorite place on the island, having stayed at the Inn several times before as guests. When they learned the Inn was for sale, they were ecstatic. Soon, they found themselves on the other side of the registration counter and in love with their new role as innkeepers.

Initially, Bob and Judy made a substantial investment in improvements. They refurbished bedrooms, modernized the kitchen, and expanded the breakfast dining. Finally, they painted inside and out. The work was not easy, but each piece of the renovation added a bit of their personality to the establishment. For them, it was a labor of love.

Throughout the project, they strived to preserve the image of the Skipjack. Not long after they opened the inn, the Tilgham Island Chamber of Commerce honored them with a Community Heritage award, recognizing their effort to maintain the historical integrity of the Skipjack Inn. From that day, Bob and Judy knew they had found a new home.

It was a short walk from the parking lot to the wooden steps of the front porch. At the top of the steps a covered veranda adorned with wicker chairs and small tables with freshly cut flower arrangements, wrapped the perimeter of the Inn. The back of the spacious porch offered a picturesque view of the Bay and fishing vessels moored at the marina. On the front, facing southwest, a series of high-back rocking chairs offered a prized view from which to view indescribably beautiful sunsets. Spend one weekend on the island and you realized why Tilgham attracted so many travelers.

As James opened the front door, he gazed ahead to the registration desk. Bob Fairbanks, the innkeeper, was working behind the desk at his computer. Now in his late fifties, Bob always sported a tan, regardless of the time of year. Today, he was wearing a bright yellow L.L. Bean Polar Tec jacket, trimmed in navy. Faded blue jeans, sweatshirt, and deck shoes completed the attire. A pair of reading glasses adorned his pleasantly weathered face.

Noting his clothes, James speculated that Bob had been working outside, which was what he enjoyed most. He loved his role as an innkeeper, but maintaining the inn was his joy—painting, plumbing, electrical, woodwork, marina repair—whatever was needed, he could do it. Bob was a "jack of all trades." Looking up, Bob smiled as he recognized his friend.

"James! Judy and I were expecting you! Where's Susan? How was the drive?"

Standing up from his chair, Bob walked around the registration desk to meet his friend. Extending his hand in greeting, they shook hands.

"Good to see you, Bob! Susan's in the car getting her things together. The drive was great! And the weather is absolutely perfect. Where's Judy?"

"She was in the kitchen a few minutes ago…baking cherry cobbler for the two of you! She's been looking forward to seeing you. How you doing? You holding up, okay?"

"Hang'n in there. All we can do right now."

"Yeah, I know it's been tough, but leave that stuff in Washington. Right now, we need to kick back a little."

It was that attitude that attracted James and Susan to Bob and Judy Fairbanks. They recognized the stress of his work and respected the need for quality time away from that environment. Without exception, they went out of their way to make James and Susan feel at home. They were great hosts and, better yet, wonderful friends.

Momentarily, the sound of someone opening the front door attracted their attention. Looking to the doorway, Bob smiled as Susan entered the room. In one hand, Susan carried a canvas tote bag and, over her shoulder, a leather purse. Pushing her sunglasses to the top of her head, she greeted Bob. "Well, hello there! How's the innkeeper these days?"

Walking from the desk, Bob approached Susan, placed his hands on her shoulders, and kissed her on the cheek. "Hey, lady! The innkeeper's is doing pretty well...for an old man. Susan, you look great, as always!"

Returning the kiss on the cheek, Susan looked around the room, noting the furniture, pictures and vase of fresh-cut flowers on the registration desk. "Gosh, everything looks so good! You and Judy have a special touch. And the veranda—it looks neat with the wicker and flowers!"

"Yeah, Judy's idea. You know, she's the one with the decorating talent. I'm just the hired help," he joked.

As the three friends exchanged greetings, Judy shouted a welcome from the hallway that connected the front office to the kitchen. "Hello? Hello!"

Judy was wore a white apron over her printed cotton dress. Dark brown hair and blue eyes complimented her slender, attractive figure. At fifty years of age, she exercised daily, walking two or three miles to stay fit.

Judy dried her hands on the apron as she entered the room. Smiling, she walked over to Susan, embraced her, and kissed her on the cheek. Then she turned and hugged James. "About time you got here! It's been too long since we've seen you," she pretended to scold.

"Judy," Susan exclaimed, smiling as she returned the embrace. "It's good to see you, too!"

"Hey," James added. "Bob tells me you're baking cherry cobbler?"

"Oh, it's nothing, just an old recipe. You don't like cherry cobbler, do you?" she teased, knowing it was one of his favorite desserts.

"Now, Judy, you know it's not nice to joke about cherry cobbler. That's a serious topic for me!"

"Made it just for you! You can have some for dessert *and* breakfast...if Susan says it's okay!"

"Yeah, we'll have to see if he behaves himself this weekend,"

Susan joked.

For the next few minutes, the friends talked, catching up on their personal lives. It was the kind of conversation that good friends have—focusing on hobbies and mutual interests.

Bob and James discussed a marine engine repair project on a boat down at the marina. Having some mechanical experience and knowledge of engines, James offered to take a look at the boat with Bob later that afternoon.

Judy and Susan talked about novels they were reading and their common interest in needlepoint. They would spend time together that afternoon while Bob and James worked on the boat. Soon, James and Susan put the stress of work out of their mind. It would be the weekend they longed for…at least, that was their hope.

* * * * * *

Hand in hand, James and Susan Wright walked along the marina dock. The night was clear and the air, crisp and cool to their skin. There was no wind. James wore his favorite leather bomber jacket, and Susan, a cotton sweater. They were relaxed and in love, savoring the final minutes of a perfect day on Tilgham Island.

As the remnants of daylight faded below the horizon, tiny celestial spheres, far removed from the intrusion of city lights, emerged timidly from the depthless sky of the universe. At first the gems appeared shy, but with each passing minute their confidence grew. By nightfall, they would sparkle brilliantly against the evening sky like a fistful of diamonds cast upon a bolt of black velvet.

Because there was no wind, the dark surface of the water inside the marina was smooth, like a shard of glass. Now and then, a school of baitfish, dodging the underwater attack from an invisible predator, leaped noisily from the mirror-like surface of the lagoon.

"It's been a wonderful day," James spoke. "I can't remember being more relaxed. I needed this!"

Susan squeezed his hand and looked at her husband. Smiling, she kissed him on the cheek. He was her man…a good man, her partner in life. She felt blessed to be so in love with him.

For twenty-five years, their high school romance deepened to a relationship of everlasting love and respect. James was an honest, hard-working man who took pride in his family and his career. Susan was the caring mother and faithful wife. Through her support, he found strength to cope with the greatest challenges a career military officer could ever face.

But his first love was his family—Susan, the children—always came first. At times, on special assignments, unable to communicate his whereabouts or what he was doing, he missed them the most. When he returned home, there was always a celebration with the kids. Susan made sure of that. The homecomings always made fond memories at times when he was most lonely.

As a child, James' family instilled in him the importance of faith, integrity, and hard work. His dad, James Sr., was a successful farmer in Calhoun County, Illinois. A product of the old school, he taught his children the value of education and a hard day's work.

When he was not in school, James and his brothers did chores on the farm with their dad. The only exception made to their work was their studies, football, and, of course, during the archery season, bow hunting. Summers and holidays were spent learning how to earn a living and enjoying life on the farm.

Early in his high school career, James was attracted to the military. It seemed to be in his blood. His father served four years in the Army, seeing duty in Korea during the 1950s. His uncle was a veteran, having served in the Marines.

At Calhoun County High, the school offered Army Jr. ROTC for juniors and seniors. James and several of his friends—most were football buddies—enrolled in the program during their junior year. James enjoyed the experience so much, he continued through his senior year.

Throughout Illinois and the mid-west, the Calhoun County High School ROTC Unit was recognized among the best. At Jr. ROTC competitions, James and his fellow cadets handily defeated the opposition, winning top awards in marching, physical fitness, marksmanship, and military procedures. Unit Commander, retired Captain William Smith, recognized James as a leader among the group and encouraged his student to consider a military career.

At the end of his senior year, James' scholastic record earned him distinction. Top scores on the SAT, coupled with a 4.0 high school G.P.A. brought recognition as Class Valedictorian, a National Merit Scholar and, his most coveted award, an appointment to West Point. For some young men, the multitude of college and career opportunities would have overwhelmed them. But for James, the decision was easy and during the summer following high school graduation, he was on his way to the Academy.

At West Point, James continued to distinguish himself. He played football for Army, excelled in the classroom, and possessed a natural ability for military strategy and leadership. During his junior year at West Point, James became intrigued with special operatives and intelligence strategies. With every opportunity, he took courses and read prolifically on the subject. Coupled with his physical prowess, he was a prime candidate to specialize in this training.

During the summer preceding his senior year, James seized the opportunity to participate in a rigorous six-week special forces field exercise. The training was intense and the physical demands difficult, but something about the program clicked with him. James finished among the top soldiers in the unit.

Upon graduation, James was commissioned 2nd Lieutenant and assigned to the 75th Ranger Regiment, 3rd Battalion, and Fort Benning, Georgia. At Fort Benning, his skill as a soldier and ability as a leader were clearly apparent. Within weeks, the battalion commander approached James about applying for advanced special operatives training in the US Delta Force. Stationed at Fort Bragg, North Carolina, the elite, highly specialized unit involves only the best soldiers in the world.

Although not officially recognized by the United States government, Delta Force and other special operatives play a key role in the US military campaign against terrorism and international conflict. Capable of quick deployment around the world, Delta Force missions are a critical, yet often unacknowledged, factor in these engagements. The program was a perfect assignment for James.

As James charted a successful military career, promotions reflected his superior performance. In time, he established a reputation as a special forces officer that became widely known. By 1990, he attained the rank of colonel and in 1991 was appointed commander of a Joint Special Operations Task Force in western Iraq. The mission was to locate and designate mobile Scud missile units as targets for Coalition warplanes.

By early 1991, several Delta Force and British SAS squadrons infiltrated western Iraq through Saudi Arabia. Moving at night and hiding during the day, they operated around Al Qaim, in the northern Scud box nicknamed "Scud Boulevard." The SAS worked the southern corridor called "Scud Alley." Both units conducted direct action missions against Iraq radar sites, convoys, and other targets.

In one nighttime mission, James and four three-man patrols, operating Fast Attack Vehicles (FAVs), mounted with .50 caliber heavy machine guns, engaged several units of an Iraq convoy. A fierce firefight ensued with the outnumbered Delta forces taking the brunt of the exchange. Two soldiers in James' squad were killed and another seriously wounded. It seemed a matter of time before James and his men would be overrun.

As the fight continued, James radioed for help, though he was uncertain if another squad was close enough to assist. When all appeared lost, another Delta squad, led by Colonel Jake Stahl, appeared in the midst of the heavy firefight.

Attacking the enemy flank from the left, Stahl drove his .50 caliber heavy machine gun mounted FAV through the heavy fire to Colonel Wright's crippled unit. The unexpected assault diverted Iraq fire long enough for James and his men to regroup. Then, in an act of courage, Stahl and his men gathered the wounded and the bodies of the two dead soldiers, all the while hammering the Iraqis with heavy fire as James and his squad retreated.

As Stahl and his squad took direct hits, he called for air support. Then, entrenched together, Stahl and Wright fended off the attackers long enough for a squadron of MH-47E Chinooks, from the 160th Special Operations Aviation Squadron (SOAR) to hit the Iraq convoy. Overwhelmed by the air strike, the enemy was quickly defeated.

At the conclusion of the special operations, the incident was recognized as one of the fiercest battles in the Delta force hunt for Iraq scud missiles. Two Delta force soldiers had been killed and several wounded, including Colonel Stahl and Colonel Wright. Stahl and his act of courage saved the lives of James and his men.

Following the Iraq conflict, in a special ceremony in Washington, D.C., Congress awarded Stahl the Congressional Medal of Honor, an honor bestowed to only the greatest war heroes and American patriots.

But for Colonel Stahl, that honor was short-lived. A year later, Stahl was found guilty and sentenced to military prison for illegal dealings, money laundering, and misuse of authority that involved corrupt government officials in several locations around the world. The arrest and charges devastated James. For years, he struggled to understand how his friend, comrade, and the man who saved his life could compromise his integrity and a stellar military career. No matter how he added it up, it simply did not make sense.

The Iraq experience brought recognition and advancement to James. Upon his return from the Gulf War, his ability as a leader led to promotions as brigadier general and major general and assignment as the commander of his home base unit, Delta Force at Fort Bragg, North Carolina.

In the mid 1990s, as the international war on terrorism escalated, James' knowledge and experience in special operations and intelligence attracted the attention of an up and coming US Senator from Ohio, George Stone. As chairman of the US Senate Intelligence Committee, Stone called on Major General Wright for input in the United States campaign against terrorism. Through their professional association, the two became respected colleagues and, over a period of time, good friends.

In 1998, Stone announced his candidacy for US President. Winning the Democratic Party nomination, he founded his platform on a strong will to fight the threat of international terrorism. Experience on the Senate Intelligence Committee convinced Stone that a new and advanced satellite global surveillance technology, appropriately dubbed *Voyeur*, should be the centerpiece of this initiative. Because of his professional relationship with General Wright and James' experience in the development of the *Voyeur* program, the Senator called upon the general for advice.

Over the course of the campaign, *Voyeur* became the major political issue. Stone's Republican opponent, California Senator Richard Davis, criticized the program, calling it a political charade, and an unproven program that would cost the international community billions of dollars. He described *Voyeur* as Stone's way of diverting attention from domestic issues and the state of the economy.

In a close election, however, Stone prevailed, convincing voters and international community that *Voyeur* would turn the tide against terrorism. Bitter in defeat, Davis vowed to hold Stone personally accountable for its outcome.

Upon election, it was no surprise that President Stone called on James to head the joint chiefs of staff and the newly formed *International Coalition Against Terrorism*. The presidential nomination easily won approval from a Congress that recognized James as one of America's outstanding military leaders.

Then came the bombings—the unexplained bombings. Now, James found himself in the middle of one of the greatest puzzles of his military career.

"James."

"Yes, love."

"James, have you thought about calling Frank?"

"Frank?"

"Yes, Frank Williams."

"Honestly, Susan, I have ...but I didn't want to bother him. He doesn't need this."

"I know, but perhaps he might have another perspective. At least an opinion from someone you trust."

"I know, but still. I just don't know. I'm still working on the protocols and system analysis. If those don't pan out…or God forbid…we have another incident, I can give him a call."

"Just an idea. You know what's best."

"I know. I appreciate what you're saying."

* * * * * *

Cinco de Mayo!
Downtown - Mexico City

By the time the truck was loaded, it was 9:00 a.m. For more than an hour Carlos, Pedro, and Miguel worked without stopping, stacking bag after bag of ammonium nitrate and fertilizer into the cargo bay of the truck. With the electronic detonator in place, the three men had transformed the vehicle into a powerful, mobile bomb capable of inflicting extraordinary physical damage.

Two days earlier, the terrorists parked the rental in an old, abandoned warehouse located in an unkempt section of downtown Mexico City. Working steadily, it took a full day for the three operatives to convert the bright yellow truck into a *City of Mexico Public Works* service vehicle replica.

Having painted the exterior a solid white, their leader Raheem hired a commercial sign painter to design a *City of Mexico* logo for the side panels of the truck. Paid in cash several times his usual fee, the artisan knew better than to ask questions or remember anything about those who hired him. With the makeover complete, the truck would be indiscernible among the countless service vehicles staged along the *Cinco de Mayo* downtown parade route.

Checking the time on his wristwatch, Carlos issued a command to Pedro and Miguel. "Amigos, we must go…andele! We have less than an hour to be in position! Start the truck. I'll lock the warehouse."

Without speaking, Pedro and Miguel moved to the cab of the truck, Miguel on the driver side, Pedro, the passenger. From a travel bag on the front seat, they removed two *City of Mexico Public Works* jump suits. Donning the uniforms, the men clipped forged ID tags to the front shirt pocket.

On the passenger side of the truck, a stack of orange parking cones had been stored on the floorboard. Taking his seat, Pedro adjusted them to create space for his feet. The seating configuration cramped his body, but the ride downtown would not take long. He would endure the discomfort for the short trip.

With Pedro and Miguel inside, Carlos moved to the rear of the vehicle and pulled the rear truck panel door down into a locked position. In less than a minute, he secured the enclosure and its volatile contents with a heavy-duty, steel-plated padlock. Having completed this task, Carlos stepped away from the truck to a position where Miguel could see him in the side-view mirror. With hand signals, he motioned him to drive through the warehouse doorway and onto the street.

Responding to the command, Miguel cranked the engine and shifted the manual transmission into gear. Pressing the accelerator carefully, the vehicle moved forward. Following close behind, Carlos pulled the metal warehouse door closed as the vehicle cleared the exit.

Miguel drove the truck down the street and made a left turn at the first intersection. Again, he glanced in the side-view mirror. There, a half block away, he watched as Carlos opened the driver door to a pickup truck parked along the warehouse curb. Miguel was to drive the pickup to a rendezvous point six blocks from where he and Pedro would park the truck filled with explosives. *So far*, Miguel thought, *everything was according to plan.*

As they approached the downtown area, the congestion of traffic and pedestrians along the parade route increased. At each intersection, a police officer directed the flow of traffic and pedestrians. By the time Miguel and Pedro reached *Paseo de la Reforma*, hundreds of parade spectators, waving flags and balloons, filled the sidewalks. On every street corner, vendors touted souvenirs, candy, and food.

Earlier that morning, to control access to *Paseo de la Reforma*, the Mexico City Police Department erected black and white striped wooden barricades along the parade route. At each check point an officer monitored vehicular access to the road.

Miguel and Pedro grew anxious as they approached the first checkpoint and made eye contact with the police officer standing in front of the black and white barrier. But their anxiety quickly vanished as the officer pulled the barricade aside, smiled, and motioned for the men to proceed. The officer had given the service vehicle and its occupants little more than cursory attention. Pedro and Miguel glanced at one another, exchanging nervous smiles as they passed the barricade.

Several blocks later, they negotiated a second checkpoint without incidence. Now, with growing confidence, the men focused their attention on the parade grandstand looming in the distance above the crowd. According to plan, they would park the truck along the curb adjacent to the platform, directly across the street from the *Palacio Nacional*.

As they approached the predetermined parking space, Miguel slowed the vehicle to a stop. Without waiting for direction, Pedro opened the passenger door, jumped to the street, and walked behind the truck. From this position, he could direct Miguel into the parking space.

Now, with less than an hour before the start of the parade, the sidewalk was filled with spectators. Laughter, music, singing, and shouting from the festive crowd filled the air. At every corner, street vendors touted their wares as they held bundles of balloons and cotton candy high above their heads. Shouting, they barked their spiel to the crowd.

On the street corner across from the *Palacio*, a small girl dressed in khaki shorts, wearing a *Cinco de Mayo* commemorative T-shirt stood patiently next to her mother. In her hand, she held a helium-filled red balloon tied to a string. Moments later, the child began to cry as she looked skyward to the spiraling sphere that had escaped her tiny grasp. Consoling her, the mother knelt down and spoke softly in her ear, attempting to appease her anguish with a bouquet of pink cotton candy.

Less than a block away, on both sides of the grandstand, parade marshals wearing red armbands and white shirts monitored the restricted area of the parade grandstand. At a designated checkpoint, an official examined VIP credentials and media passes that provided access to the viewing area. Soon, the structure would be filled with parade dignitaries, government officials, media personnel, and camera crews.

Gripping the steering wheel, Miguel focused his attention on the side-view mirror of the panel truck and the reflected image of Pedro. Touching the accelerator lightly, he followed the hand signals of his partner as he motioned him into position. Slowly, the truck backed into the parking space next to the curb. As it reached the back of the space, Pedro raised his arm with his fist tightly clinched, signaling him to stop.

Pressing the brake, Miguel double-checked the space on both sides of the truck with the side-view mirrors. Satisfied, he switched off the ignition as he pulled up on the hand lever next to the gearshift to engage the parking brake. Feeling it lock into position, he removed a cellular phone from his shirt pocket and pressed the power button. Spontaneously, the electronic device sprang to life, beeping a series of tones as it captured the relay from a nearby cell tower.

Checking its power and signal indicators, Miguel placed the cell phone on the center floorboard carpet in front of a tiny microphone that protruded from beneath the seat. A black coaxial cable connected the microphone to a receiver rigged in the center of the truck storage area. When the cell phone was activated, the microphone would transmit the telephone signal to its receiver. Thus the receiver became the detonator for the plastic explosives. Spontaneously, the detonation would ignite the truckload of explosives.

With the setup complete, Miguel pushed the door lock down, exited the vehicle, and closed the truck door. Walking to the front of the truck, Miguel took two of the orange cones from Pedro.

Despite their apprehension and feelings of self-consciousness, the terrorists collected themselves and performed their assignment precisely as Raheem had directed. To the casual observer, they were merely two city employees engaged in their daily work routine.

With the orange cones positioned at the front and back of the parking space, Miguel checked the truck one last time. Nodding his approval to Pedro, they walked shoulder-to-shoulder down the sidewalk and into the crowd.

"We must move quickly," Miguel directed quietly with his voice, "but not so fast as to attract attention."

"Si," Pedro replied. "I am with you."

Standing silently, arms folded across his chest, Mexican President Carlos Sanchez gazed wistfully out the double doorway of the veranda that overlooked the grounds of the President's residence at *Los Pinos*. His dark, black hair was combed back, slick and neatly trimmed, as was his mustache.

The President wore the full military uniform of the Mexican Army. An array of medals and colored bars splashed across the chest of his jacket reflected his status as the highest-ranking military officer in Mexico. Today, in celebration of Cinco de Mayo, President Sanchez would assume the dual role of the President of Mexico and its top military leader.

Along the open portico, flowering plants and ferns in terracotta pots adorned the expansive room. Ceiling fans, decorative chairs, and exquisite furniture, positioned carefully on the Mexican glazed tile floor, complimented the foliage. It was a relaxing environment for solitude and informal gatherings at the *Chapultepec* residence.

The clear spring morning was beautiful and the President's daily trek through the garden had been especially invigorating. It was a special day and he wanted to savor every moment.

"Senior Presidente, the motor car is ready."

Turning from the veranda to face the beckoning voice, President Sanchez recognized his staff assistant, Juanita Fuentes. Dressed in a light pastel business suit, she held the President's black brimmed military hat.

"The motorcar and driver are ready...when you are," she repeated.

"General Gonzales, his niece, and the American students are downstairs. I have your hat, sir." Smiling, she extended arm to hand him the headwear.

As he walked toward her, he took the hat and placed it carefully on his head.

"Bueno...muy bueno, Juanita. Gracias! You look very nice today. Your suit is beautiful! I like the color," he complimented as she straightened his tie and smoothed the lapels of his jacket.

"Gracias, Senior Presidente." She smiled.

Returning the gesture, the President welled with pride as he reflected on the day—the celebration of Cinco de Mayo, the opportunity to greet the American teacher and her students. With the military attire in place, the President raised his arms, extended them above his waist, and turned slowly in a pirouette for his assistant to scrutinize.

"What do you think? You say that everyone is ready?"

"Si, senior. We are ready when you are...and you look very distinguished, as always!"

The President and his assistant walked down the hallway to the stairway that led to the first floor. Moving down the steps, they could hear the voices of the students and their chaperones gathered in the foyer below. The President smiled as he listened to the excitement of their conversation. At the bottom of the stairs, he approached the group and extended his arms in a warm greeting.

"Buenos dias! Buenos dias, my American friends!"

In unison, the group of students, their teacher, and chaperones responded to the President's welcome. "Buenos dias, Senior Presidente!"

Stepping forward from the group, General Gonazales, dressed in military uniform, addressed the President.

"Senior Presidente, buenos dias!"

"Buenos dias, General!"

"Sir, it is my privilege to introduce my niece, Maria."

Maria was wearing a light cotton suit. Her black hair was slicked back, held in place with a flowered comb. As she approached the President, she extended her hand to greet him. "Senior Presidente, it is such an honor..."

"Ah...it is *my* honor, seniorita," he said, kissing her hand. "And these are your students and friends?"

"Si, senior. These are my students and friends and we are so privileged to meet you...and to participate in the Cinco de Mayo festivities."

"It is *our* privilege. America is our friend and *you* are our guests! We hope you enjoy our wonderful city and the celebration!"

Following the exchange of greetings, the President shook hands with every student and chaperone, taking the time to pose for informal photographs. Excited conversations and anticipation of the day's festivities filled the assembly.

It was the President's assistant, Juanita that kept the group on schedule.

"Senior Presidente, it is time for us to leave for the Palacio Nacional! We will assemble at that location in preparation for the parade and celebration."

"Ah, but of course, Juanita. Gracias!"

Addressing the group, President Sanchez exclaimed, "Vamos, mi amigos! We must be on our way. The festivities are about to begin!"

With the cue, the security officers, President's staff, and group of visitors moved to the motorcars parked outside the compound. Within moments, the entourage was loaded, moving swiftly from the Presidential residence to the street.

From Los Pinos, the cavalcade, led by security police officers on motorcycles with blue lights flashing, traveled downtown to Paseo de la Reforma and the Palacio Nacional. Following a brief stop for photographs at the Palacio, the Presidential party would join the mayor of Mexico City, the parade grand marshal, and other officials. Within the hour, a menagerie of decorated floats, uniformed marching bands, government officials, and dignitaries would parade the downtown streets of Mexico City like a kaleidoscope of color.

As the President's entourage approached the *Palacio*, Carlos Sanchez surveyed the gathering crowd assembled along the street. At every corner, men, women, and children smiled with pride as they raised flags and balloons at the passing motorcade. Through the protected glass motorcar window, the President waved his hand

and returned their smiles. It was a special day for Mexico.

At the front of the *Palacio*, on the sidewalk next to the street, temporary bleachers had been erected for dignitaries, parade judging, and the entourage of television and radio broadcasters. On both sides of the elevated structure, tourists and residents competed with food vendors and street entertainers for prime vantage points from which to view the parade.

Across from the *Palacio*, a group of late arriving parade participants, dressed in marching band uniforms, clutched musical instruments as they scurried to find their squad. At the barricaded parade security checkpoint, three men, wearing colorful, festive costumes, negotiated ardently with police officers for access to the staging area.

As the Presidential motorcade slowed to a stop at the street curb in front of the *Palacio Nacional*, a flock of pigeons, feeding on abandoned food items along the sidewalk, flew into the air. From the lead motorcar, six security officers, dressed in business suits and wearing sunglasses, exited from the vehicle and moved quickly to designated positions. Two of the officers approached the President's limousine and opened the door. With their assistance, President Sanchez exited the limousine, smiled, and waved to the throng of people along the sidewalk. The holiday had transformed the downtown into vibrant hub of activity.

Parked behind the President's motorcar, Maria, her students and chaperones, General Gonzales and members of the President's staff, stepped from their vehicles as the President beckoned to them. Responding to the directive, security personnel and staff assistants formed an entourage that made its way up the palace steps. With the President in the lead, the group conversed excitedly as they approached the main entrance of the Palacio. Maria walked next to the President on his right side; General Gonzales was on his left.

Moving inside the *Palacio*, the group posed for photographs at the stairway leading to the Presidential offices. On the wall, a historical mural of Diego Rivera provided an extraordinary backdrop for the photo session.

Following the photographs, the President spoke to the group as he conducted a tour of the President's offices. As he walked down the *Palacio* corridor, he recounted to Maria and her students, the history of *Cinco de Mayo* and the special significance it held for him.

"In 1861," he began, "England, France, and Spain sent troops to Mexico to collect debts owed to their governments. England and Spain took care of their affairs quickly and departed Mexico. France, however, to support its political agenda, deployed a force of troops to occupy Mexico and establish a monarchy!

"On May 5th, 1862, the Mexican Army, led by Colonel Porfirio Diaz, who, by the way, was my great-great grandfather, engaged the French and a sizable number of traitor Mexican soldiers!"

The group of visitors smiled and nodded at one another in recognition of the President's famous ancestor.

"In a decisive battle, fought at the foothills of Loreto and Guadalupe, near the city of Puebla, the outnumbered Mexican regiment defeated the formidable French Foreign Legion. Then, in 1867, when President Benito Juarez ultimately expelled the French, the battle of May 5^{th,} became symbolic of Mexico's courage against a formidable opponent. Ultimately, Cinco de Mayo became a national holiday!"

"Oh, Senior Presidente, what a wonderful story," exclaimed Maria.

"Oh, but it is my pleasure, seniorita. Now you know why this is such a special day for me!"

"And rightly so, sir. We are proud of you!"

Spontaneously, the group applauded the President.

"Gracias! Gracias! But we must go. It is time to celebrate! Andele! Andele!"

Ushering the group with his arms, the President led the entourage to the motorcars parked on the street.

* * * * * *

Pedro and Miguel walked along the side street against the stream of pedestrians that were heading to *Paseo de Reforma*. One block from the parade route, the crowd dwindled to a typical weekend flow. At three blocks, the sound of the parade festivities was little more than an indistinguishable noise in the distant background. Now, their thoughts turned to the rendezvous with Carlos.

Maintaining a steady pace, the two men were anxious to reach the security of the pickup. At the next street corner, Pedro glanced instinctively over his shoulder as though expecting someone to be following. Miguel noticed the gesture and reassured his companion.

"Hey, amigo, not to worry, everyone's at the parade! No one in Mexico City has a clue about you and me."

"Si," Pedro replied. "I'm just a little nervous, you know? I'll be glad when this thing is over...I'm heading to Rio!"

"We will all be heading somewhere soon, mi amigo! Not much longer now."

According to plan, Pedro and Miguel would meet Carlos at the predetermined parking location. From inside the truck, the three men would monitor the radio broadcast of the festivities. As the presidential party passed the parade review platform, Carlos would activate the detonator with a call to the cell phone. The electronic ring of the telephone would activate the detonator and ignite the explosives.

"There's the truck," Miguel exclaimed. "Carlos, too!"

A block ahead, parked next to the curb, was the green pickup. Carlos sat behind the driver seat, smoking a cigarette.

"Hey, I see him too," Pedro retorted. "Let's go!"

"Not so fast," Miguel commanded in a whisper, grabbing Pedro by the arm to slow him down. "Everything is fine. Be cool. We don't want to screw up...not now!"

"Sorry... I'm still nervous."

As the men approached the rear of the pickup, they tried to appear unassuming. When they reached the side of the passenger door, Pedro tapped on the window. Responding to the knock, Carlos reached across the seat and unlocked the door.

"Hey, everything okay?"

"Just like we planned," Miguel replied. "Everything's cool."

"Bueno! Get in! We don't have much time left."

Piling in the cab of the truck, the three men settled into their seats. From his shirt pocket, Carlos removed a pack of cigarettes. As he lighted the "smoke" with a match, he took a draw on the burning tobacco. Turning to his companions and extended the pack.

Without hesitation, Pedro accepted the gesture, passing the cigarettes to Miguel. Carlos struck a match for the men, who inhaled deeply on the lighted cigarettes.

As he listened to the radio broadcast, Carlos held the cell phone in his hand. With great fanfare the announcer began to describe the parade festivities. Carlos glanced at his wristwatch and noted the time: 9:50 a.m. The parade would begin in ten minutes.

Pedro, sitting between Carlos and Miguel, squirmed restlessly in his seat. Taking another deep draw on his cigarette, he leaned forward and adjusted the tuning knob on the radio. Spontaneously, Carlos slapped his hand away from the radio.

"What the *hell* are you doing, man…you trying to fuck things up? What's your problem?"

"Hey, I'm trying to make sure we have a clear signal!"

"*Clear signal!* Jesus Christ! Leave the fuckin' radio alone! We've got a clear signal, as long as you don't fuck it up!"

"Hey! Okay…okay! Sorry…just trying to help!"

"Leave the damn thing alone! It's almost time!"

The minutes ticked by slowly. Carlos looked at his watch, all the while listening carefully to the radio announcer. Then, the parade began.

"Mi amigos—seniors y senoritas—muchachas y muchachos! It is a beautiful day, a beautiful day in downtown Mexico City! A day of celebration for *Cinco de Mayo,*" exclaimed the announcer. "We begin the holiday festivities by drawing your attention to the Army flag corps approaching the review stand from my left. Today, the uniformed officers of the Presidential security unit will escort the corps on motorcycle.

"Directly behind them, our distinguished parade marshal, Mexican Presidente Carlos Sanchez.

"Chief of Staff General Gonzales, and the Mayor of Mexico City George Degas, accompany Presidente Sanchez in his limousine.

"Also, with the Presidential party, a special group from the United States, the niece of General Gonzales, American schoolteacher Maria Gonzales. Ms. Gonzales, her students and fellow chaperones, are from California. Their visit to Mexico City and participation in the *Cinco de Mayo* celebration is a school-sponsored trip. Welcome, Ms. Gonzales!"

From the open limousines, Presidente Sanchez, Maria, and her students held flags and balloons as they waved to the joyous crowd. All wore smiling faces filled with pride and the emotion of the celebration. Seconds later, the two caravans passed in front of the review stand. Simultaneously, with uncanny timing, Carlos pushed the speed dial button of the cell phone, sending its signal to the phone that now lay on the floorboard of the panel truck in front of the small microphone.

* * * * * *

Mexico City Police Officer Roberto Alvarez tipped his hat as he stepped to the side of the vegetable bin, clearing the aisle for the old woman. As she exited the open doorway of the neighborhood produce market onto the sidewalk, he greeted her with a smile.

"Buenos dias, Seniora Gomez!"

Turning to face the police officer, the old woman returned the greeting.

"Buenos dias, Roberto. Como esta"?"

"Ah, muy bien," he replied, nodding his head. "Y usted?"

"Muy bien, gracias, muy bien."

The exchange of greetings with the locals was a daily occurrence. For more years than Roberto could recall, the old downtown neighborhood near the heart of Mexico City had been his assigned beat. Every day, making his the rounds, he checked the streets, inspected the storefronts, and spoke to the residents.

Roberto was a trusted police officer. His outgoing personality, good humor, and knack for getting along with people made him popular. Everyone liked Officer Alvarez.

"May I help you with your groceries?" he asked, gesturing with his hand to the paper sack the old woman carried in the small basket attached to the frame of the four-legged crutch.

"Nada, gracias. I'm okay."

"I'll be glad to take them to your apartment," he insisted.

"No, gracias, Roberto. I do not have far to go. I can make it, gracias."

"As you wish. You be careful. ...And take it slow and easy!"

"Not to worry. I will be okay."

Gripping the handle of the aluminum-framed walker for balance, the eighty year-old woman shuffled her feet, one step at a time, along the broken, uneven surface of the sidewalk. Despite the morning heat, the senorita wore a white scarf over her hair. A loosely tied knot below her chin held the head garment in place. A white, cotton shawl that covered the back of her blue cotton dress was wrapped around her shoulders. With admiration, Roberto shook his head as he watched her slow, tenacious progress down the street.

I hope I can do that when, God willing, I'm her age, he thought, turning his attention to Julio Manuel, the storekeeper.

"Buenos dias, Julio!" Roberto shouted to be heard above the festivities.

Julio looked up from the box of vegetables at the back of the store, smiled, and returned the greeting. Julio and his wife Maria had operated the corner market for many years. Having grown up in the area, Julio saw the business as an opportunity to stay close to home and establish a career as storekeeper.

Julio and Maria worked hard to satisfy their customers. Julio personally selected the fruits and vegetables for the store and was never satisfied unless they were fresh. Vendors knew that unless they brought him quality produce, he would not do business with them. Over the years his work ethic and concern for customer satisfaction earned Julio and Maria a cadre of loyal customers. Everyone in the neighborhood shopped at *Julio and Maria's Market*.

"Roberto! Buenos dias. Como esta'?"

"Muy bien. Muy bien. I was watching senorita Gomez. She is something else! How old is she now?"

"Ah, probably eighty or so—unbelievable!"

"I was just thinking…if I can get around at that age, I'd be doing pretty good!"

"You got that right. Hey, how about a sweet roll? My Maria baked some this morning. It will be good with coffee!"

Roberto looked at his watch and noted the time—9:55 a.m.

"Almost ten." He smiled. "Just in time for my coffee break! And you *know* how much I love Maria's cooking!"

Roberto walked to the counter at the back of the store. From the shelf behind the workstation, Julio removed two powdered, sugarcoated sweet rolls from a plastic container. Julio placed them on a napkin and poured two cups of coffee from the coffee pot. Extending a steaming mug to his friend, he handed one of the pastries to Roberto. Roberto received the offering graciously. Then, like a gourmet connoisseur, he carefully inspected the roll before taking a huge bite of the powdered sugar morsel.

"These are fresh…Maria baked them this morning," Julio offered.

"Umm!" Roberto closed his eyes and moaned with exaggeration as he savored the sweet pastry. Wiping his mouth with the back of his hand, he chased the delicious treat with a gulp of black coffee.

"Julio, your Maria bakes the best rolls in Mexico," he said, taking another huge bite of the irresistible dessert. But I can only eat a couple…I have to watch my waistline, you know," he said, laughing as he patted his bulging belly.

"Oh, you can handle it! Just a few more minutes on the treadmill when you work out," Julio directed as if he moonlighted as a fitness instructor.

"Yeah, easy for you to say!"

As Roberto wiped the powdered sugar from his mouth with the napkin, he felt a concussion and the sound of the blast. Despite their distance from ground zero, the impact of the bomb shook the building like an earthquake. Instinctively, the men grabbed the edge of the counter for balance.

"What the hell was that?" Julio shouted "An earthquake?"

"No, I don't think so. I've been in an earthquake. That was an explosion! You stay put," Roberto directed. "I'll call the station! They'll know what happened."

Roberto placed the coffee mug on the counter and walked hurriedly through the doorway to the sidewalk. As he surveyed the street scene, he saw people emerge with anxious curiosity from apartments and storefronts. The scene was eerie, filled with a calm-like anxiety. Uncertain of what had happened, there was no panic among the crowd that developed along the street.

Yet ...

Earlier that morning, Roberto parked his service vehicle a block down the street. That was the starting point for his daily patrol. Now, it would serve as his post from which to respond to directives from the station. First, he had to find out what was going on.

As he turned to walk down the street, Roberto had taken only a few steps when he heard the loud sound of a racing automobile engine and squealing tires. Attracted to the noise, he looked back to see what was happening.

There, at the end of the block, the driver of a blue pick up truck, traveling at an excessive speed for the confines of the narrow street, slammed on the brakes and wheeled erratically into a vacant parking space next to the street curb. The vehicle barely stopped when three men, none of whom he recognized, emerged hastily from both sides of the truck cab.

With the driver in the lead, the two passengers jumped from the vehicle. Together, they ran down the sidewalk and around a car parked in the space near the intersection. Racing across the intersection, the men attempted to catch up with the driver of the pickup, who was now on the other side of the street.

In the hasty pursuit, the third man failed to see Mrs. Gomez hobbling across the intersection. Spontaneously, the man collided with the old woman, knocking her to the pavement. The impact tumbled the aluminum walker, the bag of groceries, its contents, and their owner onto the street.

Dazed and hurt, Mrs. Gomez writhed in pain as she moaned from a blow to her head. With little more than a cursory glance at the injured woman, the man gathered himself and continued to pursue his companions.

From the sidewalk, less than fifty feet from the intersection, Roberto watched in disbelief. Instinctively, he transformed the mental images of the street scene into a series of slow-motion still frames. Quickly, his mind recorded every detail of what was happening— the pick up truck, the men, their physical features and clothes— Roberto's brain recorded everything.

The three men were Hispanic and in their late twenties or early thirties. The first wore civilian clothes, and the other two were dressed in City of Mexico Utility Service uniforms. All three appeared nervous and scared. From the men, he focused on Mrs. Gomez, sprawled in anguish on the street.

How could he do this? Roberto thought as he watched the man continue to run, showing no regard for the old woman. Without hesitation, he raced to the intersection and shouted as he knelt down to help Ms. Gomez.

"Stop!...Policia!...Stop!"

The three men ignored his command as they continued to run.

Again, Roberto shouted. "Police officer!...Stop!"

This time, Pedro, the man who collided with Mrs. Gomez, turned and looked back to Officer Alvarez. As their eyes made contact, Roberto shouted again. "Halt! Police officer!"

But instead of complying, Pedro reached for the 9mm automatic pistol that was concealed under his shirt at the waist. Grasping the firearm, Pedro turned and fired three rounds at Roberto.

Caught by surprise, the bullets whizzed by Roberto, barely missing their mark. Instinctively, Roberto dropped to one knee as he drew his 45-caliber service automatic from its holster. In self defense, he fired at his assailant. Two of the rounds hit Pedro in the chest.

Mortally wounded, Pedro recoiled from the impact of the bullets. Disoriented and in pain, he stumbled. Then in an unconscious act, fired wildly, emptying the full clip of rounds across the intersection. All but one round missed their mark. The single bullet ricocheted off the street pavement, striking Roberto fatally in the neck. The blow knocked him back and onto the street next to Ms. Gomez.

With the exchange of gunfire, Miguel and Carlos watched incredulously as Pedro fell to the ground. As Miguel turned to assist his friend, Carlos grabbed his arm and shouted. "No! We cannot help him! He is done! We must get to Raheem…quickly! Vamos! Vamos!"

Miguel stared again at his fallen friend, then, reluctantly, turned to follow Carlos.

* * * * * *

Saturday, May 8, 2004
Tilgham Island - Chesapeake Bay, Maryland

When it first appeared, the UH-60 Black Hawk was nearly indiscernible against the midday haze of the Maryland sky. Like a tiny black gnat, the venerable chopper emerged silently above the distant horizon, hovering tempestuously toward its destination. As the aircraft approached, the pulsating cadence of its rotary blades broke the silence. With each revolution, the crescendo grew louder. Soon, the noise of its engines joined a dichotomy of sounds emerging from the powerful flying machine.

James and Susan Wright waited patiently on the grass outfield of the Tilgham Island softball field. Although they wore sunglasses, they held a free hand above their foreheads, shielding the glare of the sun from their eyes. Standing together, their arms around one another, they followed the course of the approaching chopper.

Monitoring the GPS coordinates to the rendezvous point, the pilot focused his attention on the landing area. Banking the aircraft sharply, he surveyed the ground below and identified his target. At an altitude of several hundred feet, the he cut the engine, allowing the chopper to descend deftly to the ground. Moments later, he finessed the noisy craft to a soft landing.

As the rotator slowed to idle speed, a helmeted crewmember opened the side door of the craft. A female military officer, dressed in a khaki field uniform, jumped to the ground. Struggling against the wind force of the spinning helicopter blades, she scurried to meet the General and Mrs. Wright.

Despite the prop wash, the officer followed protocol, saluting the General and shaking hands with Mrs. Wright. James returned the salute, kissed Susan on the cheek, and dashed through the strong wind to the waiting craft. Earlier, he and Susan said their "goodbyes," waiting for the transport to arrive. Now, there was work to do. The female officer would accompany Susan as they drove the Porsche back to Maryland together.

With a helping hand from the waiting crewman, James boarded the aircraft, taking his position in the jump seat behind the pilot. Reaching behind his back, he pulled the straps of the four-point safety harness over his shoulders and fastened the buckle at his waist. From the cockpit, the pilot monitored the flight preparation. With the safety harness secure, the crewman handed a flight helmet to his new passenger.

Outfitted with an internal microphone and headset, the helmet would enable the general to communicate on board during the short flight back to the Pentagon. With hand signals, the crewman gestured to the control panel above the seat. Nodding that he understood, the general connected the headset to the telecommunications system. Adjusting the volume control with his hand, the general made a voice check, then signaled "thumbs up" to the crewman. Returning the hand gesture, the crewman nodded to the pilot. Applying full power to the engines, the pilot initiated the liftoff.

As the helicopter gained altitude, James looked to the ground through the open cargo door and waved to Susan and the female officer. Standing together in the softball field, the women instinctively held on to one another against the force of the prop wash. Susan returned the wave as she walked to the red sports car parked outside the softball field chain link fence. The officer would accompany Susan back to the *Skipjack*. There she would say goodbye to Bob and Judy before returning to Washington. The weekend was nothing like she had imagined it would be.

Nodding his head, James greeted the staff officer seated across from him. The young lieutenant returned the gesture, extending a file of documents to the general, as he spoke into the headset.

"Good morning, sir."

"Good morning, Lieutenant. What the *hell* is going on?"

"Sir, it's bad—Mexico City—the Cinco de Mayo celebration. Sir, it's like the others—a bomb, no warning, no intelligence, but this time, its worse...much worse."

"Damn ... *Damn!* What are the casualties? How bad?"

"Sir, we don't have a total yet. First reports are at least 100 dead—President Sanchez and his top staffs were at ground zero. They are certain to be among the victims."

James stared in disbelief at the cockpit floor, overcome by a wave of emotion. Again, innocent lives had been lost. Shaking his head slowly, he mumbled into the microphone. "It makes no sense. None of this makes any sense."

"And, sir, there's more."

"More?" the general replied, looking at the distraught face of the lieutenant.

"Yes, sir. There are American casualties..."

"*American casualties?*"

"Yes, sir. A young, first-year high school Spanish teacher from California, her students—about twelve teenagers—and two chaperones. All of them were with the presidential party. Seems her uncle...a General Gonzales...was a key member of the presidential staff. He apparently arranged for his niece and her students to ride with the presidential party in the parade. They were on a field trip to Mexico City."

"My God!"

"Yes, sir. I understand, sir."

"Thank you, Lieutenant, I'll try to read the brief before we get back to the Pentagon." Filled with anguish, James took the report from the lieutenant. How much worse can it get, he wondered.

For a long moment, he closed his eyes, trying to collect his thoughts. Then, glancing at his watch, he calculated a mental time frame.

"It's a little before two," he directed to the lieutenant. "Call ahead and schedule a security staff meeting for 3:00 p.m. I'll contact the secretary as soon as I get to the office. Is he in Washington?"

"Yes, sir. We've been in touch with him. He wants to talk with you ASAP! All of the staffs are on notice, awaiting your orders. Everything will be arranged."

"Good. Thank you, Lieutenant."

As James read the report summary, one section caught his attention. "Lieutenant!"

"Yes, sir?"

"What's this about a shoot out with a Mexico City police officer?"

"Sir, we don't know. We don't know if there's any connection. Intelligence didn't want to take anything for granted. It appears that a Mexico City police officer was engaged in a shoot out just a few blocks from the bombing. Three unidentified assailants were involved. The police officer and one of the men were killed. That's all we have right now. They are still conducting the investigating."

"I want to know everything!"

"Yes, sir."

* * * * * *

James Wright stood silently at his desk, staring out the window of his Pentagon office. He was still dressed in the slacks and shirt he wore from the helicopter ride from Tilgham Island earlier that day. From across the Potomac River, city lights twinkled against the skyline as the evening dusk settled on Washington D.C. James was tired and filled with the fatigue of a long, stressful day. Still, his mind raced as he recounted the events that generated the same questions to the "same ole, same ole" answers.

The tedious routine was a regimen that had been going on for weeks, seemingly leading him nowhere. Now, he was growing weary...uncertain. Three terrorists attack in three months...still, no explanation, no leads...no nothing!

"Has *Voyeur* failed? Does the system work? That's what everyone wants to know. That's the question everyone wants *him* to answer, even the President. *Does the system work?*"

"Hell, right now, I don't know! Maybe it doesn't work! Maybe it *is* a failure. Maybe it's not what we thought it would be. Maybe...maybe...maybe...! Nothing made sense any more...nothing."

As James turned from the window, he collapsed, exhausted into the chair at his desk. Placing his elbows on the desktop, he cradled his head in his hands, closed his eyes, and tried to think of nothing. Right now, all he wanted was a blank mind—no brain waves, no thoughts, no nothing.

Succumbing to the self-induced trance, he began to relax. But the respite was short-lived as the telephone beeped its all too familiar ring, signaling an incoming call. Opening only his eyes, his head still cradled in his hands, he listened as the tone beeped again.

Damn, he thought. Begrudging the intrusion, he reached slowly for the receiver and answered the call. "Yes?"

"James, are you still working?"

It was Susan. She always worried about him.

"Hey there. What are you doing? When did you get home?"

"Checking on you. I got home a little while ago. I'm fine, just tired. I know you are! How'd it go today?"

"You need to ask?"

"No, not really. Just thought I'd be a little formal."

"More of the same...more questions than answers."

"When will you be home?"

"I was getting ready to leave just before you called. It shouldn't be too long."

"James."

"Yes, my love."

"James, I think you should call Frank."

"Frank?"

"Yes, Frank. You know we talked about it last night at Tilgham."

"Yeah, I know. But he doesn't need this headache."

"James, you know he won't mind your calling him. He's the best there is. No one knows *Voyeur* better than Frank. Besides, he's your friend...one of your *best* friends. If he knew how you were agonizing over this and didn't call... he'd be upset with you! You need to call him... I want you to call him! This thing is killing you!"

"I know...I know. Let me think about it."

"*Think* about it! James, there is nothing to *think about*! You need to call him. I want you to!"

"Okay, okay... I'll give him a call...tonight...I'll call him tonight...when I get home... I'll call him."

"Thanks. I love you. It's not going to hurt to talk with him. At least he can give you another perspective on this whole thing. I'll see you in a little bit."

"I'm getting ready, now... see you soon."

"Bye."

* * * * * *

James leaned back in the leather desk chair of his home office. In his hand was a glass of Jack Daniels and ice. Tipping the beverage against his lips, he savored the sweet aroma of the Tennessee whiskey. Feeling relaxed, he listened patiently to the ring of the telephone in the receiver against his ear. After the third tone, he recognized the voice of his long-time friend.

"Hello!"

"Frank?"

"Yes?"

"James Wright."

"You son of a bitch!" the voice retorted. "I'm not going to ask how you are doing. I just want to know what the *hell* are you doing? What's going on with *Voyeur*?"

"Look who's calling who an SOB," James returned the jest. "If you were so concerned, why didn't you call me? Huh?"

"Okay, you got me. How are you doing...holding up? I'm worried about you."

"Hey, I'm fine. It's tough...but I'm okay... I'm doing okay."

"It's a hell of a mess, isn't it?"

"I can't begin to tell you! Frank, it makes no sense. Nothing makes any sense. I've put a microscope on the whole system... Everything checks out, but still I know something is wrong. I just don't know what! That's why I called you."

"Me?"

"Yes, Frank. I hate to burden you with this, but…I need your help. I really need your help!"

"James, you know you can call on me…for anything. But what could I possibly do that you haven't done? You know the system as well as I do!"

"Frank, I need a fresh set of eyes. A clear mind. I need someone I can trust. I really don't know what's going on and that's what scares the hell out of me. Right now, I don't know who I can trust to figure this thing out. I'm just about burned out of ideas. I need your help."

"What do you want me to do?"

"Come to Washington…tomorrow, or as soon as you can get here!"

"Okay, James. Let me think for a minute. Okay. I'll come to Washington. You say where and when. But we should think about contacting Thomas and Wilhelm. They are the real experts. They know the technology better than either one of us. They can trouble shoot the systems, the data. I think we need them."

"Absolutely. I thought about them, but didn't know how you wanted to handle it."

"Good. Why don't I call them? They'll do it. I know they will. How do we get set up in Washington? How do we connect?"

"We have to be careful. All of this must be confidential. We just don't know what we're up against."

"I have a location just outside Washington. I'll have it set up with all the technology and support staff you want. Whatever you need, let me know. I'll call you tomorrow with the itinerary and the flight schedules. Someone from my staff will meet you at Dulles. You call Thomas and Wilhelm."

"Good. I'll give them a call."

"Frank."

"Yeah?"

"I appreciate it."

"Hey, not a problem. You'd do the same for me. Don't worry. We'll figure this thing out."

"Thanks, Frank. I'll talk with you tomorrow."

* * * * * *

Oxford, England
Oxford University

"Are you certain you have the correct number? This is Thomas Leed, *Professor Thomas Leed, Oxford, England!*"

"Hey, you old *fart*," Frank Williams grinned as he spoke into the telephone receiver to his long time friend. "You know I've got the number right! How the hell are you?"

"Just keeping you on your toes! It's good to hear from you! It's been a while, at least a couple of years since we last spoke."

"I know. I'm ashamed of myself for not staying in touch."

"I'm fine. Peggy and I are fine."

"Still in Florida, I presume?"

"Oh yes. South Beach. This is home, you know."

"And don't start about the weather...sunshine, the heat; don't even go there!"

"Well, now that you mention it. The weather has been quite warm lately. Got to keep the sunscreen on," Frank chided. "In fact, I just got out of the pool!"

"You rascal! Hasn't warmed up here yet—a little sunshine, but cool and overcast. And what do I owe the pleasure of your call? What's going on?"

"Thomas, I need your help. I've got a job for you. Actually, James Wright has a job for you...us...me, you, Wilhelm... It's *Voyeur*."

"*Voyeur*? My God, Frank. James is having a hell of a time. I've thought about him often over the last several months. And now with *Cinco de Mayo*!"

"I know. That's why I called. That's why he called me...yesterday.

He needs our help!"

"*Our* help? What can we do? He's got the best staff there is. What's going on?"

"That's what he's trying to figure out. He doesn't know, at least not at this point."

"Goodness, he's been in one hell of a mess...the bombings, the system breakdown. Now, the politics is starting to take hold."

"Exactly. That's the crux of it. He's tried everything he can to trace the problem. So far, he's found nothing. All the systems check out. Now, he's suspicious. Doesn't know whom to trust. Thomas, he's in trouble!"

"Frank, you know I'd be glad to help, to do anything for James...for you. But it's been a while. I may not be much good to you."

"I know what you mean. I'm *rusty* myself. We may have designed *Voyeur*, but like everything else, you have to stay with it to keep up. But James is in dire straits. I told him we would do what we could. I think that's all he expects—no miracles, just some help and support."

"Would there be a problem if I brought an assistant with me?"

"An assistant?"

"Yes, I have graduate student, a girl—Elizabeth Stall. As you were speaking, I thought about her. She did her master's thesis on the politics of *Voyeur*. From the time she learned of my involvement with *Voyeur*, she's been intrigued by its concept. Not only does she understand the politics, she's quite keen in technology, understands the system and is the best I've seen on a computer. She could work with me, and do what I can't do."

"Thomas, this is top level security we're talking about...as high as it gets! I don't know. It's not my call to make."

"Frank, she's good...very good. You won't have to worry about her. I accept responsibility. I'd try to go it alone, but I have to be honest. I haven't kept pace with the technology. The system design, the engineering...absolutely! It's the other I'm not sure about."

"I understand...everything you are saying. I'll check with James. It's his call to make. I know he wants you to be a part of the team. It's the security he'll be concerned about."

"Let him know I accept the responsibility. He won't have to worry about Elizabeth."

"I'll check with James and give you a call back."

"Good."

"Thomas?"

"Yes?"

"Thomas, James needs us right away—like tomorrow, if possible!"

"Wow! That's quick, but that's the way it usually is, isn't it?"

"Seems like old times!"

"Well, I'll be ready. Just let me know. I'll wait to hear from you."

"Thanks. I'll give you a call as soon as I know something."

"I'll talk to you soon."

* * * * * *

Washington, D.C.
A countryside mansion - Maryland

James Wright stood at the front door of the two-story fieldstone mansion. The winding cobblestone driveway and ivy covered stone security wall at the front entrance gave the secluded compound and its landscaped grounds the look of an affluent English farm and manor. A drizzling rain had fallen most of the day from the low, gray overcast sky that offered no hope for relief from the seemingly endless precipitation. Still, the weather was a minor distraction in his mind. Today, James was filled with an anticipation kindled by his hope to unravel the mysterious riddle of *Voyeur* and the holiday bombings.

James glanced at his wristwatch. It was 2:00 p.m. They would be here soon. The arrival flights of Frank, Thomas, and Wilhelm into Washington D.C. were scheduled for noon. It would take no more than a couple of hours to process their baggage and make the drive to the secluded home in the Maryland countryside.

For the past two days, James and a select group of staff worked secretively to establish a telecommunications and logistics center for the investigative team. State of the art technology and advanced software would provide technical support for the complex tasks that faced the investigators.

From the front door behind him, a uniformed staff assistant appeared in the half-open doorway. Leaning through the opening, the young officer spoke. "General, they are just down the road. They'll be here in a minute or two."

"Thank you, Lieutenant."

James turned his attention back to the driveway. As he listened, he detected the sound of the electronically controlled gate as it opened at the front entrance security checkpoint. Moments later, three black staff cars and their passengers approached the front of the mansion.

As the first vehicle slowed to a stop, James recognized the smiling face of Frank Williams sitting in the front passenger seat. He was in conversation with the staff driver.

Just like Frank, James thought, *never rides in the back seat. When you're with him, there's no doubt whose in charge.* James smiled as he reflected on the "take charge" personality of his friend. "Frank was probably giving the young staff officer driving directions. He chuckled softly as he watched him emerge, without assistance, from the front seat of the automobile.

Frank wore a light raincoat, jacket, and slacks. Grinning, he walked toward James, extending his arms in anticipation of a hug from his friend. "Goddamn, James! This is a hell of a rainy day to be entertaining friends in Washington. Seems you could have arranged a little sunshine for your old buddies." He laughed. "Remember, I live in the 'Sunshine State' now."

"Hey," James retorted, extending his arms to his friend. "I didn't invite your ass up here for a vacation. You *'retirees'* are going to work for a change!"

"All right, now, be careful. You'll be here with us sooner than you think!"

"Is that a promise or an offer? Right now, I'll take either one!"

The two friends embraced; their mutual respect and admiration were obvious.

"Frank," James spoke seriously. "It's good to see you. I appreciate you guys being here."

"Not a problem. Hey, you'd do the same for us. At least you better!"

From the second and third cars, two female companions and several staff assistants accompanied Thomas and Wilhelm as they walked to the front porch. The women—Elizabeth Stall and Maria Petroncelli—were the associates Thomas and Wilhelm invited to assist in the investigation. When he learned of their backgrounds,

James agreed to include them as a part of the team.

"Thomas...Wilhelm...ladies! You must be Elizabeth and Maria. Welcome. It's nice to meet you. I just wish the circumstances were different!"

"James," Thomas spoke first. "Good to see you. This is my graduate assistant, Elizabeth Stall."

"It's nice to meet you, Elizabeth. I've heard so many good things about you. Welcome to the team!"

"Thank you, sir," Elizabeth exclaimed. "I've heard great things about you, too."

"This is Maria," Wilhelm followed, introducing his friend as he shook hands with James.

"Maria. It is my pleasure. Thanks for being here. It's good to see all of you! Come inside. I know you are exhausted from the trip. We have rooms for you and there is food waiting in the kitchen! Come in...come in!"

"How were the flights?"

"Routine—direct flight from Miami—smooth and on time."

"The London flight was fine; the usual long trip over the 'Big Pond, but no problems," Thomas added as the group walked inside the mansion foyer.

At the end of the foyer, a winding staircase led to the second floor. To the left was a large living room, completely furnished. Adjacent to the living room was another large room with double doors. Floor to ceiling bookcases gave the second room the appearance of a study. A long table, lined with comfortable leather chairs, filled the center of the room. The Country-English style décor enhanced the European look of the spacious home.

On the right side of the foyer hallway, a double door-size opening led to the dining room. Beyond the dining room was the kitchen doorway. As the group cued in the foyer, James described the arrangements.

"This, obviously, is the downstairs living area. We set up the study, just beyond the living room, for your workspace. Upstairs, there are separate bedrooms and baths for each of you. The staff will assist you with your luggage and personal items.

"This is the dining room," he said, gesturing to the room to his right. "And the kitchen is just beyond, through the swinging door. Make yourself at home and feel free to raid the refrigerator any time!

"The bar, I'm talking to you, now, Thomas, is toward the back of the house, in the family room. There's liquor, beer, wine and other beverages. Please help yourself."

"I was about to ask." Thomas smiled to his friend.

"You didn't think I'd forget, did you? Hey, there may even be a little Scotch somewhere in the stash!"

"I *knew* I could count on you, James! Never a doubt in my mind." Thomas grinned.

"Around the staircase is the downstairs...actually, the basement. There is a sauna, shower and exercise room...fully equipped. It's for your use at any time.

"Well, that's what we have. If you need anything, let me or one of the staff members know. I just appreciate your being here. I mean that. It's been tough...very tough. I need your help. What am I saying? The country, if not the world, needs your help!

"What say we get you set up in your rooms? Lunch is being prepared. It'll be ready in the study when you come down. We can begin the briefing while we eat."

The group nodded in agreement as they moved to the stairway. Two staff assistants led the group of travelers as two others followed behind, carrying luggage. Frank turned to James as he approached the stairway. "James, I know I speak for the group. We're glad to be here. We'll do what ever it takes to figure this thing out."

"Thanks, Frank. I appreciate that."

* * * * * *

Frank Williams closed the report and placed it on the table next to his bed. Removing his reading glasses, he tossed them on top of the papers and leaned back against the pillow. Reaching for the table lamp, he switched off the light, sighing as he closed his eyes for the night. It had been a long day.

The debriefing by James Wright lasted through the afternoon and into the early evening. After dinner, the team retired to their rooms to review the reports that detailed the series of terrorist-like bombings in Dublin, Tel Aviv, and Mexico City. By end of the day, the team had completed their preliminary work, including a logistics plan and checklist of tasks. Still, there was much to do and the situation, more complicated than he had imagined.

It was decided that Elizabeth and Maria would fly to Mexico City to investigate the crime scene and the three assailants involved in the police officer shooting. According to the Mexico City Police report, there was no evidence that linked the men directly to the holiday parade bombing. But the circumstances were too coincidental to the *Cinco de Mayo* attack to be overlooked and the CIA knew the man killed in the shoot out for his suspected activity with Mexican terrorist cells. At this point, nothing could be taken for granted. Besides, the information was the best lead they had in the investigation.

At the mansion, Thomas and Wilhelm would utilize the operations center and its specialized technology to connect to the Voyeur database. Through this link, they would conduct a systems analysis and protocol check. The process would be time consuming, much like searching for a needle in a haystack.

In the morning, Frank would continue his dialogue with James, reviewing every document and report since the initial deployment of *Voyeur* through the attack in Mexico City. Perhaps there was something they had overlooked, some detail, or some *thing* they had not recognized before. Together, perhaps, they might begin to unravel the strange riddle of events.

But now, he needed rest—a good night's sleep, a clear mind and some lucky break to turn the investigation around!

* * * * * *

Elizabeth stepped softly down the stairs leading to the first floor of the mansion. From the foyer, she walked quietly to the back of the house and at the end of the stairwell, turned to face the basement doorway. It was 5:15 a.m. She didn't want to disturb anyone during her morning workout.

Moving her hand to the light switch on the wall, she paused as she noticed the switch was in the "ON" position. Curiously, she opened the door and peered down the stairway. Listening, she heard the sound of what appeared to be someone jogging on a treadmill. Carefully, she made her way down the stairs to the door of the exercise room. At the bottom of the stairs, she stopped to survey the room.

There, amidst an array of fitness equipment, was Maria Petroncelli jogging on a treadmill. Looking up from the machine, Maria smiled at Elizabeth. "Good morning! What gets you up this early? Don't tell me you're a *fitness nut* like me!"

"Guilty as charged," Elizabeth replied. "An old habit I can't seem to break! How 'bout you?"

"The same, but part of the job—field work gets pretty physical at times. I'm pretty much into martial arts—karate, jujitsu. It's been a good way to discipline myself and God knows, I need that!"

"Wow! That's great! I'm into *kickboxing*. Have you tried that?"

"Kickboxing! Awesome. I did a little bit, a few years ago. But once I got into the *arts*, I've stuck with that."

Elizabeth walked past Maria to a Bowflex that was set up in the center of the room. Adjusting the resistance settings, she straddled the exercise bench in front of the piece of fitness equipment. Grabbing the handgrips of the bow, she continued the conversation.

"I'm taking lessons—*kickboxing* that is."

"Lessons?"

"Yeah, at the university. There's a student fitness center on campus. We workout three times a week."

"Terrific. How's it going?"

"Well, pretty good, I guess…I knocked out my instructor last week!"

"Knocked out your instructor? I'm impressed!"

"It wasn't on purpose, or anything like that. It just, well…it just happened."

"Is your instructor okay?"

"Oh yeah. He's okay. He kind of got a 'kick' out of it, no pun intended! Really, he was sort of proud of me. But I don't think that was in his lesson plan for that session!"

"I heard that! What a story!"

"Yeah, that's my claim to fame!"

"We've got a big day ahead of us—Mexico and all, you know."

"Yeah. I'm a little nervous, but I'm glad you're with me."

"Hey, me too! We'll be fine. Besides, with your kickboxing and my karate, anyone would be a fool to take us on!"

"You've got that right. You just might call us the *Double Trouble!*"

"I like that! I like that a lot! Okay, *Trouble*, we better get busy!"

* * * * * *

Tuesday, May 11, 2004
Mexico City, Mexico

Puffs of blue smoke lingered above the tarmac as the DC-757 wheel carriage touched down at Mexico City International Airport. The landing jostle Maria Petroncelli from the nap she had taken during the three-hour flight from Dulles International. Half awake, she turned to her companion Elizabeth, still asleep in the adjacent seat. With a gentle nudge to her shoulder, she called to her. "Elizabeth, time to wake up! We're here!"

Groggy from the London-Washington "jet lag," Elizabeth responded, opening her eyes as she oriented herself. "Already?"

"Already? Girl, that was a three-hour flight! Time to wake up! You haven't got anything on me. Remember, I left Europe yesterday just like you! I've got my own case of jet lag to deal with!"

"Okay... okay...I'm awake! I'm awake. What time is it?"

"Almost noon...their time."

"Well, at least we gained a little time. What's the plan?"

"We've got customs to go through. With the heightened security, it will take longer than usual. But we've got time. No need to rush."

"I thought we'd get the rental car and check in at the hotel. We can get a little rest, then take a ride downtown. I have the directions to the apartment. By late afternoon, we should be able to get inside and have a look around."

"Sounds like a plan to me," Elizabeth replied, straightening her blouse. "Let me get my carry on. I'll be ready as soon as the aisle clears."

"I'm with you."

HAPPY HOLIDAYS: A POLITICAL THRILLER

* * * * * *

Carlos and Miguel stepped from the pickup truck, closing the doors behind them. Glancing down the street, they acted nonchalantly as they walked together along the sidewalk toward the apartment complex three blocks away.

Neither of the terrorists was excited about the assignment Raheem had given them earlier that day. Returning to the scene of the crime to retrieve the bank account ledger and safety deposit box key was *not* something they relished. With the memory of the shootout four days earlier still fresh in their mind, they knew there was a limit to how far they could push their luck. Still, the only way they would get their cut of the contract money was to recover the bank documents.

"How far are we from the apartment?" Miguel whispered under his breath.

"About three blocks. The truck will be fine parked in the alley. Besides, there's no one around. We'll come back here when we get the bankbook and key. I don't plan on hanging around any longer than we have to."

"You got that right! I'm ready to get the hell out of Mexico as soon as I get my money. Why didn't Raheem take care of this, anyway? He's the one who left the stuff in the desk! Now he sends us out to do *his* job!"

"Hey, hey, mi amigo! Take it easy! Raheem's the boss. What the boss tells you to do…you do! That's it! No questions asked. Don't forget, there was a lot going on with the shooting. He didn't have time… in all the confusion."

Without further conversation, the men moved quickly along the sidewalk, edging ever closer to their destination. Despite their anxiety, the evening twilight and deserted streets somehow comforted the two conspirators. At the intersection, across from the apartment complex, Carlos and Miguel paused to check the street. Seeing nothing to arouse their concern, the men walked cautiously to the yellow police ribbon at the foot of the apartment stairway. Since the shootout with the police officer, the pathway to their hangout had become the center of international media attention. The men stooped under the yellow band as they made their way up the stairs to the second floor...

* * * * * *

"There it is…the apartment…on the left! See…the yellow ribbon around the stairs!"

From her position in the front passenger seat of the rental car, Elizabeth Stall studied the Mexico City road map folded across her lap. Looking ahead, she compared the location marked by her index finger to the address on the street sign a half block ahead.

"Yes, this is it," she exclaimed to Maria. "Pasada Avenue! Yellow ribbon is all over the place!"

"You got it," Maria replied. "Great job, *navigator!*"

It was 6:00 p.m. and the two women were tired, but suddenly rejuvenated with their discovery. Finally, after having searched for more than an hour, they had located the crime scene where, four days earlier, the Mexico police officer had been fatally shot. Gently, Maria touched the brake, slowing the automobile as she made a right hand turn at the intersection.

"I'll park on this side street. We'll attract less attention."

With the exception of an old man walking along the sidewalk, the street was empty. Maria maneuvered the car next to the curb and shifted into "park." Switching off the engine, she turned to Elizabeth. "Take your time," she directed. "Walk slowly to the intersection and cross the street. From there we'll follow the sidewalk to the apartment stairway. When everything is clear, we'll go upstairs… quickly."

"Don't forget the shawl. Pull it around your head and shoulders. Use it as a disguise. We don't want to look like tourists!"

"Not today." Elizabeth smiled. "Besides, I don't see a shopping mall anywhere!"

"You got that right! Let's go!"

From the side street, the women exited the car and, without pausing, made their way across the intersection. Slowly, walking shoulder-to-shoulder, they ambled along the sidewalk to the apartment complex. At the base of the stairway, Maria looked back at the intersection, then ahead down the street. Two blocks away a pedestrian was walking away from where they stood.

"Clear... let's go," Maria ordered.

Together, the women shuffled up the stairs to the covered walkway that wrapped around the second floor of the apartments. At the end of the veranda was the door to the apartment that, according to the police report, was used by the assailants. On the front of the door, the City of Mexico Police Department posted a warning notice: *"No Trespassing! Crime Scene—Do Not Enter!"*

Glancing at one another, they looked around. No one in sight!

"Let's do it," Maria exclaimed, removing a small tool kit from her purse.

With the skill of a locksmith, Maria negotiated the lock and opened the door. Quickly, the women entered the apartment, closing the door behind them. As they stood quietly in the center of the room, their eyes adjusted to the dim light. Days earlier, the City of Mexico police had searched the apartment. From the disarray, the police were obviously not concerned with the mess they left behind.

"Take a look around," Maria directed diplomatically. "I don't know what's here, but perhaps we'll find something—some clue as to what's going on. If not, at least, we can mark this assignment off our list.

"I'll search the bedrooms and the living room. You take the kitchen and bath. Frank said to check everything," she continued. "The police may have overlooked something!"

"Gotcha," Elizabeth replied.

From the living room, they began the search, moving carefully through the apartment to avoid detection. Elizabeth checked the kitchen, making her way through a mound of beer bottles, broken glass, paper, and trash.

The kitchen table was strewn with food scraps and cigar butts from an overturned ashtray. Meticulously, she checked the kitchen cabinets and drawers before moving down the hall to the bathroom.

At the back of the apartment, Maria searched the bedrooms. The first was comprised of a single bed, table, and lamp. Other than a couple of coat hangers and a tattered cardboard box, the closet was empty. The second bedroom was devoid of furniture. *Nothing here,* Maria thought to herself.

Maria returned to the living room where she paused to note the arrangement of furniture—a cloth sofa, broken recliner chair, and in the corner of the room, a wooden desk, chair, and lamp. Curious, she walked to the desk and pulled open the front drawer. Carefully, she sorted through remnants of paper, a pencil, and loose paper clips. Maria closed the tray, satisfied the scraps of paper were meaningless.

Moving her hand to the top right drawer, she noted the compartment was smaller and narrower than the first. Grasping its handle, she pulled it open.

"Empty," she said to herself, peering inside. Pushing it closed, she inspected the drawer below.

The bottom drawer was larger than the top and slightly ajar. With both hands, she tugged at its handle. Grudgingly, the drawer relented. Looking inside, she examined the void space.

"Nothing," Maria exclaimed. "Not a damn thing," she cursed.

Grunting, she struggled to close the heavy drawer.

"Damn," she cursed again! "Won't close."

Exasperated, she pushed the drawer with her foot. This time, the drawer conceded, moving back to its original position inside the compartment. Stepping away from the desk, she stared sarcastically at the piece of furniture.

"Pain in the ass," she mumbled, personifying the desk.

"Hey, what's going on?" Elizabeth called from the hallway.

"Damn desk drawer wouldn't close! Finally got it, though. Any luck?"

"No, nothing. The kitchen looks like a shrine to the *Garbage Gods*!"

"Yeah, I could smell it when we first walked in."

"You ready?"

"Yeah, nothing here," Maria replied, surveying the room. "Let's get the hell out of here! We better not push our luck."

Maria walked to the front apartment door and paused as she looked back over her shoulder. With a cursory glance, she gave the living room a final inspection as she reached for the doorknob. Then, without speaking, she paused and looked back at the room again.

Turning around, Maria examined the stark walls and dilapidated furniture with her eyes. Gazing past the sofa, her eyes scrutinized the wooden desk and its cantankerous drawer. Standing quietly, with a blank look on her face, she appeared immersed in deep thought and oblivious to things around her. As she continued to stare, Maria mumbled softly under her breath. Trance-like, she stepped toward the desk and mumbled again.

"Hey, I thought we were leaving?" Elizabeth queried.

As though she did not hear the question, Maria replied, "Look at the desk. Tell me what you see."

Confused with the question, Elizabeth replied, "What?"

"Look at the desk! Tell me what you see," Maria repeated emphatically.

"What...a wooden desk... a chair! Let's go! We need to get out of here!"

"No! Look closely! See anything wrong?"

"No! What? I don't see anything...a chair...drawers... What's going on?" Elizabeth replied with exasperation, still uncertain where the questions were going.

Slowly, Maria walked to the front of the desk. "Give me a hand with the drawer."

Obediently, Elizabeth followed the directive. Standing in front of the desk, the women knelt to the floor. Together, they grasped the drawer handle. Maria turned to Elizabeth. "Ready?"

"Ready!"

"Now!"

With the queue, the women pulled forcefully on the wooden receptacle, dislodging the drawer from its compartment. As the drawer hit the floor, Maria and Elizabeth fell backward, then scrambled to sit up.

"Empty," Elizabeth exclaimed. "I thought you checked it?"
"I did! That's not what I'm looking for!"
"What then?"
"Why wouldn't the drawer close? What jammed it?"
Elizabeth turned her gaze to the void space of the desk compartment and gasped! "My God! What's that," noting a black leather, zippered envelope lying at the bottom of the opening.
"Maybe what we've been looking for," Maria replied anxiously, reaching for the leather article.
Grasping the leather case with her hands, she pulled the zipper, exposing a small ledger tucked inside. Carefully, hands shaking, she opened the booklet, examining its pages.
"This must be it! The missing link—bank account transactions and money transfers."
"Look at this," Elizabeth chimed, holding a brass key in her hand.
"What's that?" Maria questioned.
"It was inside the case, down in the bottom. Maybe from a bank deposit box?"
"Could be. Hey, we need to go. Let's get out of here! We can check this stuff out back at the hotel. I can access a software program that should tell us something about the account. Let's go!"
Pushing up from the floor to stand, the women turned to leave the apartment, then gasped as they stared at two men standing in the front doorway.
As Carlos and Miguel stepped inside the apartment, Carlos reached back to the door, pushing it closed. Looking first at Miguel, he turned to the women and smiled. "Buenos dias, senioritas," he grinned with a look of mischief. "What a pleasant surprise! Don't you agree, Miguel?"
"Si', mi amigo. Two beautiful ladies! This *is* unexpected... but *nice!*"
As they spoke, Elizabeth and Maria stepped back slowly, taking a position several feet away from the strangers. Anxiously, they exchanged glances as they stood silently, together, facing the men.
"Ah, don't be bashful," Carlos cajoled menacingly. "We won't

hurt you... just a little fun... a little affection for a couple of lonely men. You ladies know what I mean."

"Miguel, which of the two beautiful ladies do you want?"

Turning her head slightly toward Elizabeth, Maria whispered, "Which one do *you* want?"

Though the words were the same, Elizabeth knew exactly what Maria meant, and it *wasn't* what Carlos and Miguel were thinking.

"The one on the right," she responded, referring to Miguel.

Without command, Elizabeth made a quick, hop-step toward Miguel as she leapt from the floor. Simultaneously, she transformed her body in mid-air to a laid-out position. Coiling her leg, she unleashed a kick with her foot. The powerful blow hit Miguel squarely in the face.

With the impact, Miguel's head snapped backward, and his eyes rolled back in his head. Stunned by the hit, Miguel collapsed to the floor unconscious.

Carlos stared in disbelief at his fallen comrade. But the distraction made him vulnerable to Maria's swift attack. In a calculated maneuver, Maria unleashed a kick to the solar plexus of Carlos's chest. Spontaneously, the air from his lungs was expelled in an audible gasp.

Buckling at the waist, his chin became the target of Maria's second kick. With a crack, the blow snapped Carlos's head back. Losing consciousness, he fell in a heap beside his companion.

As they stood up from the floor Maria and Elizabeth exchanged glances, then smiled.

"Good job, girl," Maria chided.

"You too! Let's get the hell out of here!"

"You got that right! Grab the case. Let's go!"

* * * * * *

"Cayman Islands," Maria exclaimed as she moved her head closer to the laptop computer screen.

"Cayman Islands? What are you talking about?" Elizabeth asked as she looked at the computer screen from her standing position behind Maria's shoulder.

It was Friday evening and the women were now in their hotel room, having returned from the terrorist's apartment and their impromptu, yet triumphant, fight with the two unknown attackers. Driving back to the hotel, Maria telephoned Wilhelm to brief him on the incident. When Frank Williams received the report, he called James Wright, who, in turn, alerted the Mexico City Police officials. Now, it was likely the two hoodlums were in custody.

Through her work as an INTEPOL intelligence officer, Maria could access sophisticated intelligence gathering software. Experience told her it would not be difficult to decipher the bank account numbers listed in the registry book they recovered from the apartment. With luck, she might even identify the account holder.

As she shared this knowledge with Elizabeth, a rush of anticipation welled inside both women. Perhaps, just perhaps, they were on the verge of solving the riddle of the terrorist's attacks. When they returned to the hotel, they wasted no time in setting up Maria's laptop computer.

"Cayman Islands," Maria shouted, seeming to ignore Elizabeth's curiosity. "Cayman Islands!"

"What are you talking about?" Elizabeth repeated, still perplexed.

"The account numbers! The account numbers are from a bank in the Cayman Islands! And why should I be surprised? The Caymans are the money laundering capital of the world!"

"You're kidding! This is unbelievable," the neophyte investigator stammered. "Whose account? Is there a name on the account?"

"Yes, but it looks like some kind of organization—*Arabic National League Fund*. Never heard of it. Probably a front for a more prominent terrorist cell."

"Let's check the money transfers. I should be able to trace that also. This software is *unbelievable!*"

"I heard that! I had no idea this technology existed," Elizabeth exclaimed. "Amazing!"

"Hey, you wouldn't believe what's out there. This is primitive compared to some of the programs we have.

"Let's see," Maria mumbled under her breath as the software processed the data.

With lightning speed, frames of data blurred across the computer screen. Seconds later, the image froze on a page that resembled an account spreadsheet. Manipulating the mouse pad with her index finger, Maria performed a series of keystrokes. Finally, she stopped at what appeared to be the account header page containing demographic data. As she studied the screen, Maria mumbled under her breath. "Whew... looks like a *World Banc* account," she uttered. "Yes, it is. Most of the transfers are from a bank account in Zurich."

"How do you know that?" Elizabeth asked naively.

Turning her head slowly, Maria looked over her shoulder and stared at Elizabeth. With feigned sarcasm, she rolled her eyes, shook her head and grinned.

Catching the look, Elizabeth smiled. "Sorry...just asking!"

Maria chuckled as she turned her attention back to the computer. "Definitely a Zurich account—probably more of the money laundering scheme. I think we can trace this down though."

"Can you identify the account holder on this one?"

"Yes. In fact, we've got a name and password."

"A name?" Elizabeth exclaimed. "Fantastic! Who is it?"

"Hey, you won't believe this! How do you spell your last name?"

"Who? *Me*?" Elizabeth retorted, not expecting the question. "Stall. Elizabeth Stall. S-T-A-L-L. Why?"

"Well, this individual, whoever he is, has your last name—at least it *sounds* the same as yours! He spells it *Stahl.* S-T-A-H-L...*Jacob Stahl*. And the password...weird...Happy Holidays! *Every transaction uses that password—Happy Holidays—really weird! Now, it's beginning to connect—the password...the holiday attacks... a little sick, if you ask me!"*

With the words, Elizabeth felt as though she had been hit in the gut. Stunned, she reeled back and away from Maria.

Sensing the reaction, Maria turned to Elizabeth. Her gaze confirmed her intuition. There, several feet away, Elizabeth stood pale and expressionless, appearing dazed. Her complexion was almost colorless. Her eyes stared into space in a fixed position.

"Elizabeth? Are you okay? What is it? What's *wrong*?"

For a moment, Elizabeth was speechless, then, she mumbled quietly, slowly. "My father," she whispered. "That's my father."

"Your *father*?" Maria exclaimed. "What on *earth* are you talking about?"

"The name... you just read...the name, that's my *father's* name."

"What are you saying?" Maria replied, confused, not understanding.

"I don't know what I'm saying! I don't know... All I know is that's my father!"

Overcome with emotion, Elizabeth began to cry uncontrollably. Maria stood from her chair and embraced her friend.

"I'm sorry," Maria cajoled. "Maybe it's someone else...maybe it's a mistake!"

"No, it's no mistake," Elizabeth sobbed, wiping her eyes with the back of her hand. "It's no mistake. You just don't know. *No one knows*! No one could understand. *I* don't understand," she cried as Maria maintained her embrace.

"Tell me ... tell me about your father."

"Oh, Maria," Elizabeth continued to sob. This time she wiped her eyes with a tissue Maria had given her. "It's a long story... a very long story."

"Let's talk...just you and me," Maria nurtured. "You talk...I'll listen. Let's sit on the bed. Come..."

Maria embraced her friend as she guided Elizabeth to one of the double beds in the hotel suite. Together they sat. Moments later, holding the hand of her companion, Elizabeth shared the tragic events of her life.

"Unbelievable," Maria exclaimed after hearing Elizabeth's story. "I'm sorry, Elizabeth. I'm so...so... sorry."

"Oh, it's okay," Elizabeth replied, still sobbing, but now feeling some emotional relief. "There's nothing that can be done about it. It's just the way it is. I've learned to live with it. It's my life. I don't know anything else. I've tried to move on. I've learned to cope...but now... I just don't know."

"It will be okay. In the end, everything will work out. I believe that. *You must believe that!* Besides, we're all in this together."

"I know... I know. Oh, Maria, what would I do without you?"

The two friends embraced as they cried together.

Brushing Elizabeth's hair back with her hand, Maria looked into her eyes and smiled. "It will all work out. Don't worry," she soothed.

"Does the account give an address?" Elizabeth asked as she regained her composure. "Does it say where he lives?"

"Let's check it out," Maria replied as she moved to the desk chair in front of the computer.

Resuming her seat, she studied the screen. "Yes, it gives a Los Angeles street address: Orange Avenue! Maybe a house or an apartment... I don't know."

"Los Angeles," Elizabeth repeated. "Makes sense; that's where he was after his release from prison. At least, that was the last information I was given."

"Yeah, he's probably been staying in a familiar area...minimizing the risks and the chance of making a mistake," Maria suggested.

"Most of his life...his career, he lived in L.A. It's probably the closest thing to home for him. He traveled all over the world in the Army. But most of the time, he lived or was stationed in California."

Maria studied the data on the computer screen. As she compared the transactions between the Cayman and Zurich accounts, a chilling pattern of coincidence and conspiracy emerged. It wouldn't take a rocket scientist to connect the money trail to the holiday terrorist attacks.

"I'm going there," Elizabeth suddenly stated.

"You're going *where?*" Maria replied, still concentrating on the computer screen.

"California...L.A... I'm going there ...now!"

Maria turned quickly in her chair to face Elizabeth. *"What are you saying?"* she exclaimed. "You're going to L.A... to see your father? Are you *crazy?* What are you saying?"

"I'm going to L.A! I've got to go! I must go! I have to face him!"

"Elizabeth! What good will it do? He's not changed! It won't make any difference. Besides, it's too dangerous. Sure, you are his daughter. But he's in deep trouble now. You don't know how desperate he may become!"

"I'm going. I know you mean well, Maria, but… I have to go… for me…for Mom…for our family... I have to go! Please, Maria…you must understand!"

"I *don't* understand, Elizabeth. But I see your determination. You know I must report this to Wilhelm and Frank?"

"I know. I'm not trying to interfere with that. I just have to confront him…one last time. Before, I was a little girl. Now, I am a woman. I have to face him."

"Okay. I'm going to make the phone call. I don't know how much time they'll give you…if they give you any time at all. But…you be careful, girl. You be very careful... and call me! Do you hear?"

"I hear you. I'll be careful. Don't worry. Let me call the airline. I need to check the next flight to L.A."

"Are you going to call Thomas?"

"Yes, but after I get to the airport. I *know* what he's going to say! He'll be worried, too."

"Well, just be sure you let him know. He cares about you, just like the rest of us."

"I know... I will. I'll call him."

* * * * * *

Wednesday, May 12, 2004
Los Angeles, California

The Aero-Mexico DC 757 to LAX International Airport touched down at 6:05 p.m. The flight from Mexico City had been routine, the kind Elizabeth liked best—nothing exciting, just your basic, uneventful flight. Now, she was anxious to complete her mission.

Despite airport security processing, she cleared customs in less than an hour. After a brief stop at the restroom, Elizabeth traced the direction signs from the main concourse to the designated area for ground transportation. The trek across the terminal was a congestion of people, seemingly going in different directions at the same time.

Along the street, outside the terminal, taxi cabs and shuttle service vehicles were assigned parking space for passenger pick up. Standing at the curb, Elizabeth quickly attracted the attention of a taxi cab driver. Responding to her beckoning hand, the driver wheeled the bright yellow, four-door sedan into an empty space in front of where she was standing.

With the motor running, the cab driver shifted the taxi into park, opened the trunk, and exited the driver side door. Moving quickly to the rear of the vehicle and then to Elizabeth, the middle-aged Hispanic took the black, wheeled carry-on from her hands. Placing the luggage inside the rear compartment, he locked the trunk and opened the rear passenger door. As Elizabeth took her seat, the driver closed the door before resuming his position behind the wheel.

Turning to Elizabeth he asked. "Where are we going today, young lady?"

From her purse, Elizabeth retrieved a piece of paper, upon which she had written her father's address. Handing the shard to the driver, she replied, "This is the address."

The driver looked at the note, then asked, "Have you been there before?"

"Uh, no, sir... Is there a problem?"

"No ma'am. Just thought you might have a particular route you wanted to take. Some of my locals do. I know the location. The drive should take no more than thirty minutes."

"Thank you. I appreciate it."

Thirty minutes, she thought. *Seems like forever, but then again, so soon.* How would she handle this...confronting a father whom she had not seen since she was a little girl? He might not recognize her, not that it mattered. How long had it been? Twelve years? Twelve years—hard to believe! So much of her life was like a dream, a *bad* dream. A broken home, depressed mother; not much fun growing up.

But things changed when she graduated high school and then on to college. She was a good student, *a very good student.* Scholarships and awards opened doors of opportunity—Stanford... Oxford. In spite of the set backs, she had done well.

Elizabeth was tenacious, dogmatic... not afraid of work. Her mom was proud...as proud as she could be with her own life in shambles. But she always supported her the best she could. Mom was there. Not like her father! He abandoned them—a failure as a husband, as a father, an ex-con, and now a murderer... a terrorist? It was hard to believe her own father. She hated him...*hated* him!

What an awful thing to say about your father. What an awful thing to say! But what else *could* she say? He didn't love her. He didn't love her mother...his wife. He didn't care about anyone, except maybe... in some twisted way... himself!

No, there was nothing to say!

But tonight, what would she tell him? What words would she use? How could she express the feeling of betrayal...a lifetime of disappointment and bitterness? What would she say?

She did not know. One thing, though, when she finished...*when she finished*, her father would have no doubt who she was or how she felt about him; that, she knew!

No, it would not be easy, but it had to be done. *She* had to do it—for herself—for her mother...for all the innocent people. She had to confront him this time as an adult, not as a child.

"Ma'am!"

From the front seat, the voice of the cab driver interrupted her thoughts. As she gazed out the passenger window, fleeting images of a residential area just beyond the freeway flashed past the speeding vehicle.

Spontaneously, Elizabeth responded to his call. "Yes?"

"We are almost there. We take the next exit."

Elizabeth felt the driver slow his speed as he approached the exit ramp. "Thank you. When we get there, please wait...at the street. I won't be long. I must return to a hotel near the airport. I have a flight in the morning."

"Yes, ma'am. Whatever you wish."

Without conversation, the driver followed the exit ramp, paused briefly for traffic at a *Yield-Right-of Way* sign, and turned right onto to a four lane boulevard. Several blocks later, he changed lanes and made a left turn onto a residential two-lane street—*Orange Avenue*. Sidewalks, lined with grass and regularly spaced palm trees, bordered both sides of the narrow pathway.

This, then, was the street of her father's address.

The neighborhood was comprised of middle-income residences. The dwellings were small, modest, single-family homes built in the forties and fifties. Years ago, the subdivision was a primary residential area within the original city limits of Los Angeles. But like most urban communities, the city boundary had been extended to encompass population growth in the suburbs and outlying areas. Now, it was impossible to distinguish one community from another. Still, neighborhoods like this continued to exist indiscriminately between the suburbs and inner city.

The driver slowed the taxi as he looked for the address. Then, as he recognized the numbers on the piece of paper in his hand, he reduced his speed and pulled the taxi to the curb.

"Ma'am, this is it—the house on the right."

From the rear seat, Elizabeth recognized the address as the one she had written on the piece of paper. "Please wait. I won't be long."

"Not a problem…whatever you wish."

Elizabeth gathered her purse and opened the rear passenger door. Before closing it she leaned inside toward the driver. "Thank you."

"I will be waiting."

Nervous, yet determined, Elizabeth made her way from the street curb, up the sidewalk, to the front of the house. The lawn was freshly cut and the shrubbery, neatly trimmed. A single lamp on the wall above the doorbell illuminated the porch.

Although drawn curtains covered the front windows of the home, Elizabeth detected light emanating from what she perceived to be the living room. By all appearance, the house was occupied.

Alone on the porch, her black leather purse over her shoulder, Elizabeth paused to reflect on what was about to happen. Within the next few minutes, she would see her father—a man she hardly knew. Sadly, a man she despised…hated. She could not turn back now. It had to be done. It had gone too far. Everything had gone too far. As difficult as it would be, she had to bring closure to this episode in her life; she had to move on.

Anxious, Elizabeth pressed the doorbell, prompting a ring that lasted as long as she depressed the button. She pressed the button again, and waited.

There was movement inside. Someone was at home. She heard the sound of someone walking, then the front door unlock.

It was early evening and in the fading sunlight, the figure of a man, a tall man, emerged in the doorway. The light from inside created a silhouette, but still she recognized the steel-blue eyes, dark hair and sharp, handsome features of her father. She remembered him.

At first, he said nothing, standing quietly, looking at her in a curious sort of way. Then he spoke, as he might to a stranger. "Yes. May I help you?"

As she listened to his voice, she was overcome by something

strange. A sensation unlike anything she had experienced, something mystical, almost spiritual. She began to speak, but it was as though someone else was saying the words.

"I'm Elizabeth. Elizabeth, your daughter."

Stunned by her words, Jake Stahl studied her carefully, scrutinizing her features—her hair, her eyes—her *mother's beautiful eyes*!

Clearing his throat, he spoke again, this time more softly. "Elizabeth...Elizabeth! *Is it you*? Is something wrong? Is it your mother?"

As she fixed her eyes on his, Elizabeth felt a strangeness welling inside—strong, powerful, furious—surging like a rogue wave. Her response was spontaneous, unscripted, flowing from the depth of her emotions. "*Wrong*?" she said. "*Wrong*? Oh, yes, there's something wrong all right! Not mother, it's more than that—*much* more!"

Shaken, he struggled to speak. "What are you saying?"

"*What am I saying? What am I saying? I'm saying that I hate you! That I despise you*! Look at what you did to mother and me! You were never there, never there...*never*! *But* oh! You took care of yourself, always doing *your* thing!

"Look at what it got you—a broken family...prison... your career!"

"Elizabeth, please. Come inside. Let's talk. I can explain everything."

"Inside? Explain? I don't think so...*never!* There *is* no way to explain what you are, what you've become...you...you...murderer...terrorist...those innocent people! I hate you! *I hate you!*"

"What are you saying?" he asked, finally raising his voice.

"Don't pretend with me. I'm not a child. All you've ever done is pretend!"

"Please, Elizabeth. Let's talk...please!"

From her purse, Elizabeth removed the copied pages from the Swiss bank account. Folding them, she shoved them at her father. Instinctively, he grabbed the papers as she pushed them into his chest.

"Dublin. Tel Aviv. Mexico City. Try and explain this, you...you bastard!"

With that, Elizabeth turned and walked hurriedly to the waiting taxi.

Overwhelmed with emotion, tears filled her eyes. From behind, she heard him call her name. Ignoring the appeal, she continued to walk. Then, halfway to the street, stopped and turned to him. "Oh, and by the way... *Happy Holidays!*"

Turning away again, Elizabeth walked hurriedly to the taxi, opened the rear passenger door, and climbed inside. As the door closed, the driver touched the accelerator as he sped down the street.

Alone on the porch, Jake Stahl followed the fleeting vehicle with his eyes, watching it disappear around the corner of the next block. Gathering his senses, he unfolded the papers in his hands. Carefully, he studied the documents.

There were three pages. The first page was a bank account cover statement listing his name, the Los Angeles street address, and an account number. He recognized the account—his account a *World Banc* in Zurich, the one he inherited from his father.

The second page listed transactions—four and five figure deposits and three, six figure bank wire transfers:

March 12, 2004:   *$500,000 - Dublin*

April 1, 2004:   *$500,000—Tel Aviv*

May 1, 2004:   *$750,000—Mexico City*

The third was a document he recognized. It had been a long time, but he would never forget the format of a CIA security intelligence report. The computer-generated page was produced by highly classified software whose access was among the most carefully guarded in all of DC. Within the Agency, only top security clearance staff was authorized to use the sophisticated program.

During his special operatives unit assignment, Jake used the software to gather intelligence on government officials, money laundering schemes, and other illegal financial transactions.

Although the data was streamlined, it provided compelling information:

datacode:usa/defensedept/cia/intel/rpt./rstrictaccess

World Banc, Zurich, Switzerland
Account Holder: Jacob Stahl
Address: 4823 Orange Avenue
Los Angeles, California 90001
USA
User Name: Jake Stahl
Password: Happy Holidays
Pin: 1944

Data code: PIN required for Intel options.

If Elizabeth had this information, there were others. Now it was a matter of time...they would come for him, just like before. Everything... just like before! James Wright. He had to talk to James Wright. There was not much time left...he had to talk to James Wright.

* * * * * *

Saturday Evening, May 15, 2004
CNN Headline News Studio, Atlanta

CNN Headline News Anchor Kathy Thomas noted the studio cue, looked directly at the television camera, and began her report. "Good evening, I'm Kathy Thomas reporting for *CNN Headline News* in Atlanta.

"Today, a top suspect in the international terrorist holiday bombings was arrested in California. One week to the day from the *Cinco de Mayo* attack in Mexico City, FBI and local law enforcement officers arrested Jacob Stahl, a former US Army Colonel and convicted felon, at a residence in Los Angeles. Reporting live from Los Angeles is Richard Hamilton."

Following the lead-in, the television image shifted to a news reporter standing on the sidewalk in front of a modest brick home in residential setting. It was early evening in California, near sunset. The television journalist began his report.

"Kathy, about an hour ago, FBI and law enforcement officers raided the home you see in the background, arresting a former US Army intelligence officer, Jake Stahl. In 1992, Stahl was convicted by a military court and sentenced to 10 years in prison for misconduct involving his assignment as commander of an Army special operatives unit. Two years ago, he was released, having served his time.

"Now, officials say he may be the mastermind behind a series of international terrorists bombings in Dublin, Tel Aviv, and Mexico City. At the center of the attacks is the apparent failure of *Voyeur*, the global satellite intelligence system to intercept the planned acts of terrorism."

During the live report, the television image shifted to taped video scenes of the bombings in Dublin, Tel Aviv, and Mexico City. As the reporter described the system, an animated picture depicting the satellite system is displayed on the television screen.

"From its inception, *Voyeur* was touted as a state-of-the art technology marvel capable of tracking terrorist communiqué and thus preventing the kind of attacks that have occurred this year. In recent weeks, during his reelection bid, President George Stone, a staunch proponent of the system, has come under heavy attack by critics and political opponents.

"Ironically, Stahl's capture followed an investigation in Mexico City by a special team of intelligence officers working under the direction of Chief of Staff Chairman General James Wright. It was evidence discovered by the team that led officials to this location in California."

The television image returns to reporter Richard Hamilton.

"The fact that it took traditional investigative work to break the case adds fuel to the attack political pundits are making against the President. Certainly it will be a major issue during the reelection campaign."

"As for Stahl, he is being held in the Orange County jail and where he awaits arraignment, probably on Monday morning. Reporting live from Los Angeles, this is Richard Hamilton."

* * * * * *

The orange juice tasted sweet to his lips, concentrate. *Not the real thing,* he thought, curiously, *but what did I expect coming from a prison kitchen? I don't think so.* Still, it was what he needed. Tilting his head, Jake Stahl raised the paper carton with his right hand and poured the cool, golden elixir down his throat.

It had been two days since his imprisonment at the Orange County, California jail, where he awaited arraignment on felony charges before the federal district court. At precisely 8:50 p.m., ten minutes before the nine o'clock bedtime curfew, a uniformed guard dispensed the nighttime beverage to the prisoners on the maximum-security wing. Each time, in a methodical manner, the guard passed the small container of liquid through a narrow rectangular opening in the cell door. The small passageway provided limited access to each prisoner without requiring the guard to open the cell door. Accustomed to the regularity of prison schedules, Jake could anticipate its delivery.

Today had been a long day. Now, he was exhausted. Throughout the morning, federal prosecutors had interrogated him, recording statements and making notations as they worked systematically through a litany of questions. The session seemed endless and, having been through the experience in the past, the routine held few surprises. Most of the questions were transparent and easily predictable.

Later in the day, he met with his court-appointed defense attorney. For more than two hours, they reviewed the pre-trial process and the statement he would make to the federal judge the next day. The arraignment was scheduled for 9:00 a.m. and, according to the plan, Jake would plead "not guilty" to charges of committing terrorist acts, including murder, espionage and treason. Following the plea, the judge would set a pre-trial court date and venue. Given the tight security and international media attention, the proceedings would be nothing less than extraordinary.

Standing in the center of his cell, Jake took note of his surroundings. Not surprisingly, the cellblock was dauntingly familiar. But then again, there is little variety in the security features of prisons. The cell was located at the end of a long hallway, separated from other prisoners by a secondary cellblock door.

The small, rectangular room contained a single cot, toilet, and small table, chair and wastebasket. Steel reinforced concrete walls and a metal plated door defined the boundaries of his confinement. Dim lighting throughout the wing provoked even the slightest sensation of claustrophobia. A uniformed guard was posted at the end of the hall on the outside of the second cellblock door. Every four hours, the duty shift rotated.

Prison life is a dismal environment—cold and impersonal. Not a place of opportunity or hope. For ten years, Jake Stahl lived one day at a time as he endured its hostilities. Two years ago, upon his release from Leavenworth, he vowed never to endure it again.

After the first swallow, Jake paused briefly, then, with a single gulp, consumed the 8 ounces of liquid. As he moved the container from his lips, he wiped his mouth with the sleeve of his orange prison uniform.

From the center of the cell he turned to the wastebasket and tossed the empty carton into the receptacle. Walking across the room, he sat down in the chair by the table. Within seconds, he felt the tingling sensation pulsate through his body. With each heartbeat, the powerful drug coursed through his veins, making its way to his vital organs. As the symptoms intensified, he held his head in his hands. Seconds later, he encountered the first wave of blacking out.

Spontaneously, like a flashback from years of military training in special ops, he sensed the speed and deftness with which an overdose of lethal drugs consumes the body. Having witnessed the effects firsthand, he knew there was little time remaining before he blacked out.

In front of him, on the table, was a small notepad and pencil. Earlier in the day, he used the writing instruments to record his meeting with the public defender. Trembling, he grasped the pencil with the fingers of his right hand and attempted to write. Struggling against the siege of mental darkness, he hastily scrawled his message on the pad. Completing the task, he relaxed his grip on the pencil, allowing it to fall on the table.

From the notepad, he tore a single page and, with both hands, folded it carefully. Clutching the shard of paper, he gripped it tightly in the palm of his hand.

Instinctively, he grasped his throat as he struggled to breathe. Now, the sensation was an invisible constriction that enveloped him. Perspiring heavily, he gasped, as his breathing grew shallow. Moments later he blacked out, falling to the floor of the cell.

Lying unconscious, the rhythm of his breathing became increasingly erratic. Within seconds, following several brief convulsions, it stopped completely.

For another minute, his heart continued to beat, the pulse, weak and irregular. Then, with a slight fibrillation, there was silence. At 9:05 p.m., Army Colonel Jacob "Jake" Stahl was dead.

* * * * * *

Monday, May 17, 2004
The Maryland home of James Wright

Moments before the telephone rang, James' fatigued body conceded the sleepless battle with his restless mind. It was 1:00 a.m., Monday.

Throughout Sunday afternoon and late into the evening, James had worked in his Maryland home office, immersed in intelligence reports and security briefs that detailed the transactions and contract payments made the during the terrorists bombings. Susan was in bed next to him, asleep, having turned off the television hours earlier.

Earlier that evening, as James compared the transaction entries in the ledger found by Maria and Elizabeth to the dates of the bombings, an unconscionable plan of horror and destruction unfolded. Still, the report generated more questions than answers.

Who was involved besides the two flat-footed accomplices arrested by the police at the apartment in Mexico City, that is? Neither possessed the capacity to conduct a campaign of international terrorism. What about the money? More than a million dollars in transactions; was all of this from Stahl's account? Who else was involved? What was the motive? None of it made sense.

Reaching for the telephone on the table next to the bed, he lifted the telephone receiver from its cradle and responded to the call. "Hello?"

"General?"

"Yes!"

"Sir, I'm sorry to disturb you, but it's urgent."

The caller was his top military staff assistant, a lieutenant who had been with him since the general's appointment to the Pentagon post. Often, he was assigned the arduous task of giving the general bad news. It was the lieutenant who made the calls about Dublin, Tel Aviv, and Mexico City. No one was more sensitive to the general's personal life. When he called, it was important.

"I understand, Lieutenant."

"Sir, it's about Jake Stahl."

"Jake Stahl? Yes. He's in the Orange County, California jail waiting arraignment Monday morning."

"Sir, Jake Stahl is dead!

The words hit James like a powerful blow to the gut—almost incomprehensible! James sat up in bed.

"Repeat," the general stuttered incredibly.

"Sir, Jake Stahl is dead... suicide."

"My God! Suicide? How?"

"Sir, I just received the call a few minutes ago. I don't have all the details, but the report says a guard found him when he made his evening bed check of the prison cells. Apparently, a drug overdose. We don't know the drugs or how he got them, but that's the preliminary report."

"And you're certain it was suicide?"

"Yes, sir. They found a note in his hand."

"A note?"

"Yes, sir, a note. And if I might say…a little strange."

"What did it say?'"

"Well, sir, that's what was strange. I mean, what it said…the note. It said 'Happy Holidays!'"

"It said what? 'Happy Holidays? Is that what you said?"

"Yes, sir, 'Happy Holidays!' That was it. It makes no sense, at least, no one on this end understands it. What do you think?"

James Wright did not respond to the lieutenant. Now, sitting on the edge of the bed, he repeated the words to himself as his mind raced back in time. "Happy Holidays…Happy Holidays…Happy Holidays..." Suddenly, a cold chill ran through his body. He began to perspire. Now, he understood…everything. "My God! Oh, my

God," he stuttered incredulously.

"Sir," the anxious voice of the lieutenant queried. "Are you okay?"

"Sir?" the lieutenant repeated. "Sir?"

With his hand shaking, James placed the telephone back in its cradle.

"My God!"

* * * * * *

The ring of the telephone startled Frank Williams from his deep sleep. Fumbling in the darkness, he located the handset on the lamp table next to his bed. Sitting up, he placed the receiver to his ear and mumbled. "Hello?"

"Frank, I'm coming over. You need to wake Thomas and Wilhelm."

"Jim? My God! What time is it?" Reaching for the power switch, he turned on the lamp and looked at his wristwatch. "It's 1:30 a.m.! What the hell is going on? We're flying home first thing this morning!"

"I'm coming over," James replied, appearing to ignore the question. "I'll be there in an hour. I know who did the bombings—the terrorist attacks!"

"Hell, we all do ... Stahl, and he's locked up!"

"No, Frank, Stahl's dead! He was framed! It's not him."

"My God, Jim! What the hell is going on?"

"I'll explain when I get there...wake the others!"

"Will do. I'll see you in an hour."

* * * * * *

Tuesday, May 18, 2004
Washington, D.C. - The Pentagon

Joint Chiefs of Staff Vice Chairman General Douglas Wood tapped lightly on the door. Without waiting for a reply, he entered the Pentagon office of his superior officer.

"James, Paula said that you wanted to see me."

Although it was mid-morning, the room was dimly lit with little evidence of work being done. James Wright sat quietly in the leather executive-style chair, facing away from his desk. Leaning back, he stared out the office window, arms and hands folded across his lap. Hearing the general's voice, he swiveled the chair to face the visitor.

"Good morning," the general greeted. "Paula said that you wanted to see me," he repeated

James Wright did not reply. There was only silence. Confused, the general sensed that something was wrong…that something had happened.

As the officer walked toward the desk, James Wright leaned forward in his chair, placing his arms with hands folded, on the desktop. Without speaking, he stared quietly at the general.

"Is everything okay ... what's going on?"

Maintaining his silence, James continued to stare, thinking about the character of the man standing before him. Stone-faced, his jaw tightened. Then, with a measured tone, he looked at the officer and spoke, "*Happy Holidays*, General!"

Not expecting the response, the general repeated James' words as a question. "*Happy Holidays*? What's going on, Jim?" His voice sounded anxious.

"Happy Holidays," James repeated. "Why don't you tell me?"

"I don't follow you, Jim. I don't get the point."

Irritated, James personalized his remarks. "Cut the crap, Douglas! I'm talking about the attacks—the bombings—Dublin, Tel Aviv, Mexico City ... *That's* what I'm talking about…*'Happy Holidays'*!

"Jake Stahl is dead. Now, it's you and me. Only you and I know the meaning of *'Happy Holidays'*.

"Jake knew, and *you knew*, he knew! That's why you murdered him! Well, when he figured it out… when *we* figured it out, it was too late, but we figured it out."

"What the *hell* are you are talking about, James? What's *wrong* with you? You've made a mistake," the general countered, backing away from the desk. "What's this is all about?"

"No, Douglas, it's *you* who made the mistake…*you*! Everything fits. Now, it makes sense. Back when we conducted the *Happy Holidays* operative with the CIA. You, me…Jake… he and I …we always wondered why we never could take out the target, never could get the 'top man'—the 'hit'! Dublin. Tel Aviv. Mexico City—the *main man* always seemed conveniently absent from the holiday celebration, as though he *knew* we were coming. We even asked you! You shook your head, pretended. Never could figure it out…until now!

"*You* were the one who was 'on the take'! *You*, all along, not Jake! He was your scapegoat. *He* took the fall …to prison. You used him, destroyed him…the life of a good man!"

"I don't know where you think you're going with this, but I've heard enough!"

"Oh, but, Douglas, you're just *beginning* to hear about it! The bank account… the money transfers… the *'Happy Holidays'* password, everything! But tell me, Douglas, why? Why the innocent victims? What could be worth that?"

Feigning his composure, the general stared back at James. Slowly, his complexion changed. Uncontrollably, the selfish greed of his character took hold as the paleness of his complexion rose to a blood-filled fury. Suddenly, the rage and ruthless temperament hidden inside exploded! "You *son-of-a-bitch!*" he shouted. "You think you've got it figured out! Well, maybe…maybe not. We'll see!

"Yeah, you, Jake, and me were the ones who knew the *Happy Holiday code*! It worked back in special ops and," boasting with a devilish laugh, "it works now!"

Placing both hands on the front of the desk, the general leaned forward, looking down at James. "Why? You want to know *'why'*? *I'll* tell you *'why'*! You…and Jake! The two of you! Always taking the glory. Always getting the promotion …the medals…the rank…you! *You* always had to be the one…*never* me!

"Well, I've had fuckin' enough of it! Enough, do you hear, you bastard! Damn you …damn Stahl. Now, it's my turn! When Davis becomes President, I get *your* job! You're the one who'll be 'suckin'' up! But this time, let *me* know how it feels for a change!"

"Oh, so that's how Davis fits…that was the deal—launder his campaign money…pay the terrorists…make *Voyeur* appear to fail! Stone's out… Davis is President… and you… *you* become chief… *That* was the plan!

"Clever, Douglas… very clever…*except one thing!*"

"Yeah, what's that?"

"You got caught!"

"Prove it…try and prove it, you bastard! Everything still leads back to Stahl!"

From the side of the room, the general was distracted as he heard the sound of the adjacent office door open. Turning to look, his face paled as he watched Frank Williams, Thomas Leed, and Wilhelm Rulf enter the room. In disbelief, he stared, speechless, as the three former associates approached him. The general had worked with the three special operative officers throughout his career, including the time he conducted the *Happy Holidays* operative.

"Good morning, Douglas. *Happy Holidays*," Frank Williams greeted sarcastically.

"Yes, Douglas," Thomas Leed chimed. "Long-time-no-see!"

The general stood silently, in shock, facing the men. Nervously, his heart raced as he began to perspire.

"Oh, Douglas," Wilhelm spoke, displaying a CD in his hand. We *can* prove it… *everything*! A bit of a challenge at first… and I congratulate you on that. But we can prove it!"

Thomas smiled at Wilhelm, nodding his head in agreement. Expressionless, the professor stared at the general as Wilhelm continued.

"Erasing the disks...pretty clever, Douglas! You knew your staff would not question your taking the responsibility for those files. You were their superior officer... the vice chair of the chiefs! Who would question that?"

"Soooo," Thomas continued the dissertation. "You erased...at least you *thought* you erased...the files...the conversations."

Frank Williams picked up the dialogue. "But you underestimated us, Douglas—these three old codgers standing before you. We had a 'back-up' system. Not everyone knew. Even your boss didn't know the program. But you left footprints, Douglas... and the tracks lead straight to you!"

With the CD in his hand, Wilhelm walked toward the desk. "James, what do you say we give the general a sample? The first track will be fine."

James took the CD from Wilhelm. Opening one of the desk drawers, he pushed the power button to a small technology control unit. Inserting the disk in the device, he pushed the "play" button as he adjusted the volume control. Moments later, they listened as the machine played the general's recorded telephone call to Senator Davis:

"I thought we agreed you would not call me at my office, much less use this number! It's too much of a risk!"

"Relax. Everything is fine! Everything is fine!"

"Maybe, but I don't want you using this number! Besides, what's up?"

"We need to make a money transfer soon."

"Already? When?"

"Not for a couple of weeks, but you need to line things up. Everything must be in place by the end of the month. That's the agreement."

"How much this time?"

"Seven-fifty."

"Seven-hundred-fifty thousand! Jesus Christ! That's more than we paid for Cinco de Mayo! What's going on?"

"Look, I know...I know. Al Queda gets the job done, but they don't work cheap, particularly if we score on Sanchez. Besides, you're the one who wants to be President!"

"How much more is this going to cost? We never talked this kind of money! I've got to be careful!"

"This will do it. With the money you've raised, your campaign account can handle it. It will never be missed. The people handling the transfer will make it appear to have come out of nowhere."

"Still, we need to be careful. No more phone calls! I'll have the money. We'll handle it like before."

"Just like before...just like before! Oh, by the way, Happy Holidays, Senator...I mean... Mr. President!"

As the conversation ended, James pushed the control button to stop the recording. From behind the desk, he stood up from his chair and faced the general. *"Happy Holidays,* General."

From the adjacent office door, three uniformed US Army Military Police officers entered the room. The officer in charge, a lieutenant, stepped forward, saluted General Wright, and introduced himself.

"General, sir, Lieutenant Michaels, reporting."

"Thank you, Lieutenant."

"General Woods, you are under arrest... for murder, treason, and acts of terrorism against the United States."

"Lieutenant, read him his rights...and take him with you."

The three MPs approached the general and handcuffed him. As they led the general away, the lieutenant recited the Miranda warning to their prisoner.

Shocked and in disbelief, the general glanced over his shoulder at James Wright as he exited the room.

* * * * * *

11:00 a.m. Tuesday, May 18, 2004
Atlanta - CNN Headline News

CNN Headline News anchor Karen Wood sat poised in her news desk chair, waiting for the studio queue light to turn green. Seeing the prompt, she looked directly at the camera and began her report. "This is a special CNN News report. Less than an hour ago, in an extraordinary turn of events surrounding the international terrorist bombings, Joint Chiefs of Staff Vice Chairman General Douglas Wood was arrested and is awaiting charges that he conspired to mastermind the attacks.

"Just as startling is the simultaneous arrest of Presidential candidate Senator Richard Davis at his Maryland residence as the alleged co-conspirator in the plot. First reporting live from the Pentagon is CNN News reporter Jack King."

"Good morning, Karen. These developments are truly unbelievable...unthinkable! Just a short time ago, inside the Pentagon office building behind me, Joint Chiefs of Staff Vice Chairman James Wood was arrested by military police as one of the masterminds behind the international holiday bombings that have occurred over the last several months!

"Wood's arrest coincides with that of his alleged co-conspirator, California senator and Presidential candidate Richard Davis and one day after of what, at first, appeared to be the suicide death of a primary suspect in the bombings, former Army Colonel Jake Stahl. As previously reported, Stahl was found dead in his Orange County, California prison cell where he awaited a court appearance in Los Angeles, previously scheduled for this morning. Now, officials believe the apparent suicide may, in fact, be murder!

"The arrest of the general and his alleged co-conspirator Presidential candidate, Senator Richard Davis, is one of the most extraordinary events in recent American history. How this will impact international affairs and the Presidential campaign is the centerpiece of this story. Linda?"

"Thank you, Jack. We'll go back to you in a moment, but first, *CNN Headline News* reporter Linda Ferrell has the report from Senator Davis' home in Maryland. Linda?"

* * * * * *

Washington, D.C.
Arlington National Cemetery

Countless rows of white grave markers stood like sentinels against the gentle roll of the Arlington National Cemetery hillside. In the midst of the solemn field, a young woman, dressed in a black suit stood silently in front of a wreath of white carnations, trimmed with red and blue ribbon. Two small American flags, crossed at the staffs, crowned the distinctive floral arrangement.

From the driveway near the graveside, a man, dressed in a United States Army uniform, adorned with full regalia, walked slowly toward the young woman. In his right hand, he carried a letter-size package. Hearing his footsteps, she looked over her shoulder at the approaching officer. As he drew near, she extended her hand, which he grasped as he reached her side. Standing together, hand in hand, they stared silently at the grave marker. It was Elizabeth Stall and James Wright.

For more than a minute, they stood quietly, each lost in their thoughts and prayer. Then, James turned to Elizabeth and spoke. "He was a good man, a great soldier, and father. He was a good man."

Tears welling in her eyes, Elizabeth nodded her head. "Yes, General, he was a very good man..."

Elizabeth's voice cracked as she began to cry. "Oh, God! I'm sorry! I'm so sorry," she cried.

"It's not your fault, Elizabeth. There was no way for you to know...for anyone to know. Each of us is as much a victim as the innocent people who died in this tragedy."

"But I just wish that somehow I could make it up to him. To tell him I'm sorry. "

"Elizabeth, you are a good person...a wonderful daughter. I know your dad is proud of you. I know he wishes he could be here with you—to hold you...embrace you...to tell you how much he loves you.

"We live in difficult times where the lives of good men like your father become a twisted tale, told in a story of hate, greed, and the quest for political gain. Sometimes, Elizabeth, when there is a hero among us, their presence is so uncommon that we fail to recognize them for who they are and what they mean to us. In so doing, we destroy that hero. We bring him down—try to make him one of us—something a hero can never be. Your father was a hero!"

"Always remember, Elizabeth, heroes are bigger than life, more than mortal men. Their life is *their* legacy. Their legacy...*is* the story. Now, you have the opportunity to tell your father's story—*his* legacy. One day, who knows what this will mean to you or whose lives he will touch."

With both hands he grasped the package he held under his arm and extended it to Elizabeth. "When your father was arrested in California, we found this package at his home. It's addressed to you and your Mom. There's a letter inside...and his first *Congressional Medal*. It's for you. He wanted you to have it."

Elizabeth's hands shook nervously as she took the package. Lifting its cover, she removed the folded letter. Handing the box to the general, she began to read the words of her father. Soon, her eyes welled with tears:

May 12, 2004

My dearest Sarah and Elizabeth,

For the past twelve years, my shattered life has been filled with anguish, anger, and fear. But as much as I have endured, I cannot compare this experience to the pain and disappointment you have been forced to bear. Please know the regret I feel for all that has happened and how much I wish I could lift this burden from your lives.

I want you to know that my love for you has never changed. Fond memories of when we were together have given me the strength to persevere and the will to live. Had it not been for you, I would have given up on life a long time ago.

As difficult as it may be for you to believe, I have never done anything wrong. Never would I commit the despicable acts for which I have been accused. I must believe that one day the truth will be made known and the integrity of our family name will be restored.

When that day comes—and it will come—we may not be together in body, but our spirit and love for one another will live on.

I have been blessed to have you in my life. I could never imagine a wife or daughter—a family more wonderful.

I love you always,

Jake (Daddy)

Folding the letter, Elizabeth turned to the General and embraced him. As she cried against his shoulder, he patted her back gently in comfort. "My dad...he *was* the greatest! He *is* a hero!"

"Why don't we go see your Mom. She needs you now."

"Thank you, General. Thank you so much."

* * * * * *

11:00 a.m. - Atlanta, Georgia
CNN Headline News Studio

At 11:00 a.m. in Atlanta, *CNN Headline News* anchor Carol Chaffey began her report:

"Today, at a special assembly of Congress, former Army Colonel Jacob Stahl, now deceased, was posthumously awarded the *Congressional Medal of Honor* and the rank of Major General. The *Medal* is the second award for Stahl, who earned his first for valor during the Gulf War fourteen years ago. Receiving the awards on his behalf were his former wife Sarah and their daughter, Elizabeth."

"Earlier this year, Stahl was exonerated of espionage and treason charges following the arrest and conviction of former Vice Chairman of the Joint Chiefs of Staff Douglas Wood and a co-conspirator, former California Senator Richard Davis. Woods and Davis are now in federal prison, where they await sentencing, following their convictions for terrorism, espionage, treason, and murder."

"Federal prosecutors seek the death penalty for both men."

" Reporting live from Capitol Hill is *CNN Headline News* reporter John Michaels."

"John?"

"Thank you, Carol. Just a short time ago, at a special ceremony, Congress..."

* * * * * *

Cape Hatteras, North Carolina
The Outer Banks

Barefoot, the young man and woman walked together along the beach. The surf was blue and clear as it rolled its foamy hand against the clean white Carolina sand. With the changing tide, the crescendo of the waves increased as the surf responded to the strengthening pull of the lunar gravity.

Beating with their wings against the steady breeze, sea gulls dove to the water, skimming along the line of breakers. Greedily, the airborne scavengers picked at baitfish and other morsels that floated on the undulating ocean surface. The antics were part of a futile attempt to fill their gluttonous, insatiable appetites.

Holding hands between the couple, dressed in a green bathing suit and white T-shirt, was their six-year-old son Jacob. It was July, and the mid-summer sun was blazing its relentless heat along the North Carolina coastline. The weekend trek from Fort Bragg to the coast was a family ritual whenever school and work schedules permitted.

The man was tall and, by appearance, in excellent physical condition. Short, dark hair and a deep tan defined his handsome, masculine features. Although he wore a bathing suit and white T-shirt, the Army Ranger insignia across the front of the shirt and the silver dog tags hanging from his neck distinguished him as a member of the Armed Services Special Forces unit.

As they made their way along the shoreline, the young woman gazed lovingly at her husband and smiled. Both seemed relaxed and preoccupied with their son, who routinely broke free of their grasp to pick up one of the countless seashells strewn along the sandy beach. With each "discovery," the little boy shouted in excitement as he handed the prize to his Dad.

"Here's another one, Daddy!"

Feigning astonishment, the young father exclaimed approval as he placed the shell inside the plastic pale he carried in his free hand. Now, the growing pile of seashore artifacts nearly filled the container.

"Hey, Jake, that's a good one! See if you can find one more. I think there's still a little room left in your bucket!" Looking at his wife, Elizabeth, he smiled as he thought about the innocence of his child's world.

As he grasped their hands again, the little boy called to his mother. "Mommy, tell me the story about Papa!"

"The story about your Papa? And what story would that be?" she replied.

"Mom! You know the one—when Papa fought those bad guys in the desert with the machine-gun. He saved everybody's life and he won the medal! You know the one! Tell her, Daddy. *You* remember what Papa did! You know the story!"

"Oh yes, Jake! I remember! *Everyone* remembers your Papa. He was a hero…everybody's hero. A real *G.I. Joe!* Your mom will tell the story…"

"Just like my *G.I. Joe?*"

"Just like your *G.I. Joe!*"

"Papa is my hero, too! One day, Daddy, I'm going to be just like you and Papa! I'm going to be a *G.I. Joe!*"

"Okay, guys, if you insist," Elizabeth exclaimed, pretending to concede! "I'll tell the story…*again!*"

"Once upon a time, long before you were born, your Papa…"

* * * * * *

Printed in the United States
25999LVS00001B/290